IAN WATSON

"Perhaps the most purely brilliant of the new SF writers of the Seventies . . ."
—Fantasy & Science Fiction

"One of the few around who is not afraid to use the new sciences of communication as well as the old ones of technology . . ."
—The London Times

"The most interesting British sf writer of ideas . . . he writes a heady, zest-filled prose that whips up a froth of speculation . . ."
—J.G. Ballard

THIS YEAR'S WINNER OF THE BRITISH SCIENCE FICTION ASSOCIATION'S AWARD

Here is a collection of his most exciting stories, stories bound to take you to the outer edges of reality . . . and beyond.

D1211143

THE VERY SLOW
TIME MACHINE

BY IAN WATSON

SF
ace books
A Division of Charter Communications Inc.
A GROSSET & DUNLAP COMPANY
360 Park Avenue South
New York, New York 10010

THE VERY SLOW TIME MACHINE

Copyright © 1979 by Ian Watson

An ACE Book
by arrangement with Victor Gollancz Ltd.

Cover art by Paul Alexander

First Ace printing: April 1979

Printed in U.S.A.

ACKNOWLEDGMENTS

The Very Slow Time Machine first appeared in Anticipations edited by Christopher Priest, 1978.

Thy Blood Like Milk first appeared in New Worlds Quarterly, 1973.

Sitting on a Starwood Stool first appeared in Science Fiction Monthly, 1974.

Agoraphobia, A.D. 2000 first appeared in Andromeda 2 edited by Peter Weston, 1977.

Programmed Love Story first appeared in Transatlantic Review, 1974.

The Girl Who Was Art first appeared in Ambit, 1976.

Our Loves So Truly Meridional first appeared in Science Fiction Monthly, 1974.

Immune Dreams first appeared in Pulsar 1 edited by George Hay, 1978.

My Soul Swims in a Goldfish Bowl first appeared in The Magazine of Fantasy & Science Fiction, 1978.

The Roentgen Refugees first appeared in New Writings in SF 30 edited by Ken Bulmer, 1978.

A Time-Span to Conjure With first appeared in Andromeda 3 edited by Peter Weston, 1978.

On Cooking the First Hero in Spring first appeared in Science Fiction Monthly, 1975.

The Event Horizon first appeared in Faster Than Light: an original anthology about interstellar travel edited by Jack Dann and George Zebrowski, 1976.

The lines of verse in The Event Horizon (31 lines from "Diwan over the Prince of Emgion" and 6 lines from "The Tale of Fatumeh") are from Selected Poems by Gunnar Ekelöf, translated by W. H. Auden and Leif Sjöberg. Copyright © Ingrid Ekelöf, 1965, 1966. Translations copyright © W. H. Auden and Leif Sjöberg, 1971. Reprinted by permission of Penguin Books Ltd.

For Nell and Bill Watson

CONTENTS

The Very Slow Time Machine 1

Thy Blood Like Milk 31

Sitting on a Starwood Stool 71

Agoraphobia, A.D. 2000 82

Programmed Love Story 89

The Girl Who Was Art 96

Our Loves So Truly Meridional 107

Immune Dreams 121

My Soul Swims in a Goldfish Bowl 140

The Roentgen Refugees 148

A Time-Span to Conjure With 167

On Cooking the First Hero in Spring 190

The Event Horizon 207

THE VERY SLOW TIME MACHINE

(1990)
The Very Slow Time Machine—for convenience:
the VSTM*—made its first appearance at exactly
midday 1 December 1985 in an unoccupied space
at the National Physical Laboratory. It signalled
its arrival with a loud bang and a squall of ex-
pelled air. Dr. Kelvin, who happened to be looking in its direction, reported that the VSTM did
not exactly spring into existence instantly, but
rather expanded very rapidly from a point source,
presumably explaining the absence of a more
devastating explosion as the VSTM jostled with
the air already present in the room. Later, Kelvin
declared that what he had actually seen was the
implosion of the VSTM. Doors were sucked shut
by the rush of air, instead of bursting open, after
all. However it was a most confused moment—
and the confusion persisted, since the occupant of
the VSTM (who alone could shed light on its
nature) was not only time-reversed with regard to
us, but also quite crazy.

*The term V S T M is introduced retrospectively in view of our
subsequent understanding of the problem (2019).

One infuriating thing is that the occupant visibly grows saner and more presentable (in his reversed way) the more that time passes. We feel that all the hard work and thought devoted to the enigma of the VSTM is so much energy poured down the entropy sink—because the answer is going to come from him, from inside, not from us; so that we may as well just have bided our time until his condition improved (or, from his point of view, began to degenerate). And in the meantime his arrival distorted and perverted essential research at our laboratory from its course without providing any tangible return for it.

The VSTM was the size of a small station wagon; but it had the shape of a huge lead sulphide, or galena, crystal—which is, in crystallographer's jargon, an octahedron-with-cube formation consisting of eight large hexagonal faces with six smaller square faces filling in the gaps. It perched precariously—but immovably—on the base square, the four lower hexagons bellying up and out towards its waist where four more squares (oblique, vertically) connected with the mirror-image upper hemisphere, rising to a square north pole. Indeed it looked like a kind of world globe, lopped and sheered into flat planes: and has remained very much a separate, private world to this day, along with its passenger.

All faces were blank metal except for one equatorial square facing southwards into the main body of the laboratory. This was a window—of glass as thick as that of a deep-ocean diving bell—which could apparently be opened from inside, and only from inside.

The passenger within looked as ragged and tattered as a tramp; as crazy, dirty, woe-begone and
tangle-haired as any lunatic in an ancient Bedlam
cell. He was apparently very old; or at any rate
long solitary confinement in that cell made him
seem so. He was pallid, crookbacked, skinny and
rotten-toothed. He raved and mumbled sound-
lessly at our spotlights. Or maybe he only
mouthed his ravings and mumbles, since we
could hear nothing whatever through the thick
glass. When we obtained the services of a lip-
reader two days later the mad old man seemed
to be mouthing mere garbage, a mishmash of
sounds. Or was he? Obviously no one could be
expected to lip-read backwards; already, from his
actions and gestures, Dr. Yang had suggested that
the man was time-reversed. So we video-taped the
passenger's mouthings and played the tapes
backwards for our lip-reader. Well, it was still
garbage. Backwards, or forwards, the unfortunate
passenger had visibly cracked up. Indeed, one
proof of his insanity was that he should be trying
to talk to us at all at this late stage of his journey
rather than communicate by holding up written
messages—as he has now begun to do. (But more
of these messages later; they only begin—or,
from his point of view, *cease* as he descends further into madness—in the summer of 1989.)

Abandoning hope of enlightenment from him,
we set out on the track of scientific explanations.
(Fruitlessly. Ruining our other, more important
work. Overturning our laboratory projects—and
the whole of physics in the process.)

To indicate the way in which we wasted our

time, I might record that the first "clue" came from the shape of the VSTM which, as I said, was that of a lead sulphide or galena crystal. Yang emphasized that galena is used as a semiconductor in crystal rectifiers: devices for transforming alternating current into direct current. They set up a much higher resistance to an electric current flowing in one direction than another. Was there an analogy with the current of time? Could the geometry of the VSTM—or the geometry of energies circulating in its metal walls, presumably interlaid with printed circuits—effectively impede the forward flow of time, and reverse it? We had no way to break into the VSTM. Attempts to cut into it proved quite ineffective and were soon discontinued, while X-raying it was foiled, conceivably by lead alloyed in the walls. Sonic scanning provided rough pictures of internal shapes, but nothing as intricate as circuitry; so we had to rely on what we could see of the outward shape, or through the window—and on pure theory.

Yang also stressed that galena rectifiers operate in the same manner as diode valves. Besides transforming the flow of an electric current they can also *demodulate*. They separate information out from a modulated carrier wave—as in a radio or TV set. Were we witnessing, in the VSTM, a machine for separating out "information"—in the form of the physical vehicle itself, with its passenger—from a carrier wave stretching back through time? Was the VSTM a solid, tangible analogy of a three-dimensional TV picture, played backwards?

We made many models of VSTMs based on

these ideas and tried to send them off into the past, or the future—or anywhere for that matter! They all stayed monotonously present in the laboratory, stubbornly locked to our space and time.

Kelvin, recalling his impression that the VSTM had seemed to expand outward from a point, remarked that this was how three-dimensional beings such as ourselves might well perceive a four-dimensional object first impinging on us. Thus a 4-D sphere would appear as a point and swell into a full sphere then contract again to a point. But a 4-D octahedron-and-cube? According to our maths this shape couldn't have a regular analogue in 4-space, only a simple octahedron could. Besides, what would be the use of a 4-D time machine which shrank to a point at precisely the moment when the passenger needed to mount it? No, the VSTM wasn't a genuine four-dimensional body; though we wasted many weeks running computer programs to describe it as one, and arguing that its passenger was a normal 3-space man imprisoned within a 4-space structure—the discrepancy of one dimension between him and his vehicle effectively isolating him from the rest of the universe so that he could travel hindwards.

That he was indeed travelling hindwards was by now absolutely clear from his feeding habits (i.e. he regurgitated), though his extreme furtiveness about bodily functions coupled with his filthy condition meant that it took several months before we were positive, on these grounds.

All this, in turn, raised another unanswerable question: if the VSTM was indeed travelling backwards through time, precisely where did it *disappear* to, in that instant of its arrival on 1 December 1985? The passenger was hardly on an archaeological jaunt, or he would have tried to climb out.

At long last, on midsummer day 1989, our passenger held up a notice printed on a big plastic eraser slate.

CRAWLING DOWNHILL, SLIDING UPHILL!

He held this up for ten minutes, against the window. The printing was spidery and ragged; so was he.

This could well have been his last lucid moment before the final descent into madness, in despair at the pointlessness of trying to communicate with is. Thereafter it would be *downhill all the way*, we interpreted. Seeing us with all our still eager, still baffled faces, he could only gibber incoherently thenceforth like an enraged monkey at our sheer stupidity.

He didn't communicate for another three months.

When he held up his next (i.e. penultimate) sign, he looked slightly sprucer, a little less crazy (though only comparatively so, having regard to his final mumbling squalor).

THE LONELINESS! BUT LEAVE ME ALONE!
IGNORE ME UNTIL 1995!

We held up signs (to which, we soon realized, his sign was a response):

ARE YOU TRAVELLING BACK THROUGH TIME? HOW?
WHY?

We would have also dearly loved to ask: WHERE
DO YOU DISAPPEAR TO ON DECEMBER 1 1985? But
we judged it unwise to ask this most pertinent of
all questions in case his disappearance was some
sort of disaster, so that we would in effect be
foredooming him, accelerating his mental breakdown. Dr. Franklin insisted that this was nonsense; he broke down *anyway*. Still, if we *had*
held up that sign, what remorse we would have
felt: because we *might* have caused his breakdown and ruined some magnificent undertaking.
. . . We were certain that it had to be a magnificent undertaking to involve such personal sacrifice, such abnegation, such a cutting off of oneself from the rest of the human race. This is about
all we were certain of.

(1995)
No progress with our enigma. All our research is
dedicated to solving it, but we keep this out of
sight of him. While rotas of postgraduate students
observe him round the clock, our best brains get
on with the real thinking elsewhere in the building. He sits inside his vehicle, less dirty and di-
shevelled now, but monumentally taciturn: a
trappist monk under a vow of silence. He spends
most of his time re-reading the same dog-eared
books, which have fallen to pieces back in our
past: Defoe's *Journal of the Plague Year* and
Robinson Crusoe and Jules Verne's *Journey to the
Centre of the Earth*; and listening to what is pre-

sumably taped music—which he shreds from the
cassettes back in 1989, flinging streamers around
his tiny living quarters in a brief mad fiesta
(which of course we see as a sudden frenzy of
disentangling and repackaging, with maniacal
speed and neatness, of tapes which have lain
around, trodden underfoot, for years).

Superficially we have ignored him (and he, us)
until 1995: assuming that his last sign had some
significance. Having got nowhere ourselves, we
expect something from him now.

Since he is cleaner, tidier and saner now, in this
year of 1995 (not to mention ten years younger)
we have a better idea of how old he actually is;
thus some clue as to when he might have started
his journey.

He must be in his late forties or early fifties—
though he aged dreadfully in the last ten years,
looking more like seventy or eighty when he
reached 1985. Assuming that the future does not
hold in store any longevity drugs (in which case
he might be a century old, or more!) he should
have entered the VSTM sometime between 2010
and 2025. The later date, putting him in his very
early twenties if not teens, does rather suggest a
"suicide volunteer" who is merely a passenger in
the vehicle. The earlier date suggests a more mature researcher who played a major role in the
development of the VSTM and was only prepared
to test it on his own person. Certainly, now that
his madness has abated into a tight, meditative
fixity of posture, accompanied by normal activities such as reading, we incline to think of him
as a man of moral stature rather than a time-

kamikaze; so we put the date of commencement of the journey around 2010 to 2015 (only fifteen to twenty years ahead) when he will be in his thirties.

Besides theoretical physics, basic space science has by now been hugely sidetracked by his presence.

The lead hope of getting man to the stars was the development of some deep-sleep or refrigeration system. Plainly this does not exist by 2015 or so—or our passenger would be using it. Only a lunatic would voluntarily sit in a tiny compartment for decades on ends, ageing and rotting, if he could sleep the time away just as well, and awake as young as the day he set off. On the other hand, his life-support systems seem so impeccable that he can exist for decades within the narrow confines of that vehicle using recycled air, water and solid matter to 100 per cent efficiency. This represents no inconsiderable outlay in research and development—which must have been borrowed from another field, obviously the space sciences. Therefore the astronauts of 2015 or thereabouts require very long-term life support systems capable of sustaining them for years and decades, up and awake. What kind of space travel must they be engaged in, to need these? Well, they can only be going to the stars—the slow way; though not a very slow way. Not hundreds of years; but decades. Highly dedicated men must be spending many years cooped up alone in tiny space-craft to reach Alpha Centaurus, Tau Ceti, Epsilon Eridani or wherever. If their surroundings are so tiny, then any extra payload costs prohibitively. Now

who would contemplate such a journey merely
out of curiosity? No one. The notion is ridiculous—*unless* these heroes are carrying something
to their destinations which will then link it in-
exorably and instantaneously with Earth. A tachyon descrambler is the only obvious explanation. They are carrying with them the other end of
a tachyon-transmission system for beaming material objects, and even human beings, out to the
stars!

So, while one half of physics nowadays grap-
ples with the problems of reverse-time, the other
half, funded by most of the money from the space
vote, pre-empting the whole previously extant
space programme, is trying to work out ways to
harness and modulate tachyons.

These faster-than-light particles certainly seem
to exist; we're fairly certain of that now. The main
problem is that the technology for harnessing
them is needed *beforehand*, to prove that they do
exist and so to work out exactly *how* to harness
them.

All these reorientations of science—because of
him sitting in his enigmatic vehicle in deliberate
alienation from us, reading *Robinson Crusoe*, a
strained expression on his face as he slowly ap-
proaches his own personal crack-up.

(1996)
If you were locked up in a VSTM for X years,
would you want a calendar on permanent
display—or not? Would it be consoling or taunting? Obviously his instruments are calibrated—
unless it was completely fortuitious that his jour-

ney ended on 1 December 1985 at precisely midday! But can he see the calibrations? Or would he prefer to be overtaken suddenly by the end of his journey, rather than have the slow grind of years unwind itself? You see, we are trying to explain why he did not communicate with us in 1995.

Convicts in solitary confinement keep their sanity by scratching five-barred gates of days on the walls with their fingernails; the sense of time passing keeps their spirits up. But on the other hand, tests of time perception carried out on potholers who volunteered to stay below ground for several months on end show that the internal clock lags grossly—by as much as two weeks in a three month period. Our VSTM passenger might gain a reprieve of a year—or five years!—on his total subjective journey time, by ignoring the passing of time. The potholers had no clue to night and day; but then, neither does he! Ever since his arrival, lights have been burning constantly in the laboratory; he has been under constant observation. . . .

He isn't a convict, or he would surely protest, beg to be let out, throw himself on our mercy, give us some clue to the nature of his predicament. Is he the carrier of some fatal disease—a disease so incredibly infectious that it must affect the whole human race unless he were isolated? Which can only be isolated by a time capsule? Which even isolation on the Moon or Mars would not keep from spreading to the human race? He hardly appears to be. . . .

Suppose that he had to be isolated for some very good reason, and suppose that he concurs in his own isolation (which he visibly does, sitting there reading Defoe for the nth time), what demands this unique dissection of one man from the whole continuum of human life and from his own time and space? Medicine, psychiatry, sociology, all the human sciences are being drawn into the problem in the wake of physics and space science. Sitting there doing nothing, he has become a kind of funnel for all the physical and social sciences: a human black hole into which vast energy pours, for a very slight increase in our radius of understanding. That single individual had accumulated as much disruptive potential as a single atom accelerated to the speed of light—which requires all the available energy in the universe to sustain it in its impermissible state.

Meanwhile the orbiting tachyon laboratories report that they are just on the point of uniting quantum mechanics, gravitational theory and relativity; whereupon they will at last "jump" the first high-speed particle packages over the C-barrier into a faster-than-light mode, and back again into our space. But they reported *that* last year—only to have their particle packages "jump back" as antimatter, annihilating five billion dollars' worth of equipment and taking thirty lives. They hadn't jumped into a tachyon mode at all, but had "möbiused" themselves through wormholes in the space-time fabric.

Nevertheless, prisoner of conscience (his own conscience, surely!) or whatever he is, our VSTM passenger seems nobler year by year. As we move away from his terminal madness, increasingly what strikes us is his dedication, his self-sacrifice (for a cause still beyond our comprehension), his Wittgensteinian spirituality. "Take him for all in all, he is a Man. We shall not look upon his like. . . ." Again? We shall look upon his like. Upon the man himself, gaining stature every year! That's the wonderful thing. It's as though Christ, fully exonerated as the Son of God, is uncrucified and his whole life re-enacted before our eyes in full and certain knowledge of his true role. (Except . . . that this man's role is silence.)

(1997)

Undoubtedly he is a holy man who will suffer mental crucifixion for the sake of some great human project. Now he re-reads Defoe's *Plague Year*, that classic of collective incarceration and the resistance of the human spirit and human organizing ability. Surely the "plague" hint in the title is irrelevant. It's the sheer force of spirit, which beat the Great Plague of London, that is the real keynote of the book.

Our passenger is the object of popular cults by now—a focus for finer feelings. In this way his mere presence has drawn the world's peoples closer together, cultivating respect and dignity, pulling us back from the brink of war, liberating tens of thousands from their concentration camps. These cults extend from purely fashionable manifestations—shirts printed with his face, now neatly shaven in a Vandyke style; rings and worry-beads made from galena crystals—through the architectural (octahedron-and-cube meditation modules) to life-styles themselves: a Zen-like "sitting quietly, doing nothing."

He's Rodin's *Thinker*, the *Belvedere Apollo*,
and Michelangelo's *David* rolled into one for our
world as the millenium draws to its close. Never
have so many copies of Defoe's two books and the
Jules Verne been in print before. People memorize
them as meditation exercises and recite them as
the supremely lucid, rational Western mantras.

The National Physical Laboratory has become a
place of pilgrimage, our lawns and grounds a vast
camping site—Woodstock and Avalon, Rome and
Arlington all in one. About the sheer tattered
degradation of his final days less is said; though
that has its cultists too, its late twentieth-century
anchorites, its Saint Anthonies pole-squatting or
cave-immuring themselves in the midst of the
urban desert, bringing austere spirituality back
to a world which appeared to have lost its
soul—though this latter is a fringe phenomenon;
the general keynote is nobility, restraint, quiet
consideration for others.

And now he holds up a notice.

I IMPLY NOTHING. PAY NO ATTENTION TO MY
PRESENCE. KINDLY GET ON DOING YOUR OWN THINGS. I
CANNOT EXPLAIN TILL 2000.

He holds it up for a whole day, looking not
exactly angry, but slightly pained. The whole
world, hearing of it, sighs with joy at his modesty,
his self-containment, his reticence, his humility.
This must be the promised 1995 message, two
years late (or two years early; obviously he still
has a long way to come). Now he is Oracle; he is
the Millennium. This place is Delphi.

The orbiting laboratories run into more difficulties with their tachyon research; but still funds pour into them, private donations too on an unprecedented scale. The world strips itself of excess wealth to strip matter and propel it over the interface between sub-light and trans-light.

The development of closed-cycle living pods for the carriers of those tachyon receivers to the stars is coming along well; a fact which naturally raises the paradoxical question of whether his presence has in fact stimulated the development of the technology by which he himself survives. We at the National Physical Laboratory and at all other such laboratories around the world are convinced that we shall soon make a breakthrough in our understanding of time-reversal—which, intuitively, should connect with that other universal interface in the realm of matter, between our world and the tachyon world—and we feel too, paradoxically, that our current research must surely lead to the development of the VSTM which will then become so opportunely necessary to us, for reasons yet unknown. No one feels they are wasting their time. He is the Future. His presence here vindicates our every effort—even the blindest of blind alleys.

What kind of Messiah must he be, by the time he enters the VSTM? How much charisma, respect, adoration and wonder must he have accrued by his starting point? Why, the whole world will send him off! He will be the focus of so much collective hope and worship that we even start to investigate Psi phenomena seriously: the concept of group mental thrust as a hypothesis for his mode of travel—as though he is vectored not through time of 4-space at all but down the waveguide of human will-power and desire.

(2001)

The millennium comes and goes without any revelation. Of course that is predictable; he is lagging by a year or eighteen months. (Obviously he can't see the calibrations on his instruments; it was his choice—that was his way to keep sane on the long haul.)

But finally, now in the autumn of 2001, he holds up a sign, with a certain quiet jubilation:

WILL I LEAVE 1985 SOUND IN WIND & LIMB?

Quiet jubilation, because we have already (from his point of view) held up the sign in answer:

YES! YES!

We're all rooting for him passionately. It isn't really a lie that we tell him. He did leave relatively sound in wind and limb. It was just his mind that was in tatters. . . . Maybe that is inessential, irrelevant, or he wouldn't have phrased his question to refer merely to his physical body.

He must be approaching his take-off point. He's having a mild fit of tenth-year blues, first decade anxiety, self-doubt; which we clear up for him. . . .

Why doesn't he know what shape he arrived in? Surely that must be a matter of record before he sets off. . . . No! Time can not be invariable, determined. Not even the Past. Time is probabilistic. He has refrained from comment for all these years so as not to unpluck the strands of time past and reweave them in another, undesirable way. A tower of strength he has been. *Ein' feste Burg ist unser Zeitgänger!* Well, back to the drawing board, and to probabilistic equations for (a) tachyon-scatter out in normal space (b) time-reversal.

A few weeks later he holds up another sign, which must be his promised Delphic revelation:

I AM THE MATRIX OF MAN.

Of course! Of course! He has made himself that over the years. What else?

A matrix is a mold for shaping a cast. And indeed, out of him shapes have been molded increasingly since the late 1990s, such has been his influence.

Was he sent hindwards to save the world from self-slaughter by presenting such a perfect paradigm—which only frayed and tattered in the Eighties when it did not matter any more; when he had already succeeded?

But a matrix is also an array of components for translating from one code into another. So Yang's demodulation of information hypothesis is revived, coupled now with the idea that the VSTM is perhaps a matrix for transmitting the "information" contained in a man across space and time (and the man-transmitter experiments in orbit redouble their efforts); with the corollary (though this could hardly be voiced to the enraptured

world at large) that perhaps the passenger was not
there at all in any real sense; and he had never
been; that we merely were witnessing an experiment in the possibility of transmitting a man
across the galaxy, performed on a future Earth by
future science to test out the degradation factor:
the decay of information—mapped from space on
to time so that it could be observed by us, their
predecessors! Thus the onset of madness (i.e., information decay) in our passenger, timed in years
from his starting point, might set a physical limit
in light-years to the distance to which a man
could be beamed (tachyonically?). And this was
at once a terrible kick in the teeth to space
science—and a great boost. A kick in the teeth, as
this suggested that physical travel through interstellar space must be impossible, perhaps because of Man's frailty in the face of cosmic ray
bombardment; and thus the whole development
of intensive closed-cycle life-pods for single astronaut couriers must be deemed irrelevant. Yet a
great boost too, since the possibility of a receiver-
less transmitter loomed. The now elderly Yang
suggested that 1 December 1985 was actually a
moment of lift-off to the stars. Where our passenger went then, in all his madness, was to a
point in space thirty or forty light-years distant.
The VSTM was thus the testing to destruction of a
future man-beaming system and practical future
models would only deal in distances (in times) of
the order of seven to eight years. (Hence no other
VSTMs had imploded into existence, hitherto.)

(2010)

I am tired with a lifetime's fruitless work; how-

ever, the human race at large is at once calmly
loving and frenetic with hope. For we must be
nearing our goal. Our passenger is in his thirties
now (whether a live individual, or only an epi-
phenomenon of a system for transmitting the
information present in a human being: literally a
"ghost in the machine"). This sets a limit. It sets a
limit. He couldn't have set off with such strength
of mind much earlier than his twenties or (I sin-
cerely hope not) his late teens. Although the teens
are a prime time for taking vows of chastity, for
entering monastries, for pledging one's life to a
cause. . . .

(2015)
Boosted out of my weariness by the general
euphoria, I have successfully put off my retirement for another four years. Our passenger is now
in his middle twenties and a curious inversion in
his "worship" is taking place, representing (I
think) a subconcious groundswell of anxiety as
well as joy. Joy, obviously, that the moment is
coming when he makes his choice and steps into
the VSTM, as Christ gave up carpentry and
stepped out from Nazareth. Anxiety, though, at
the possibility that he may pass beyond this critical point, towards infancy; ridiculous as this
seems! He knows how to read books; he couldn't
have taught himself to read. Nor could he have
taught himself how to speak in vitro—and he has
certainly delivered lucid, if mysterious, messages
to us from time to time. The hit song of the whole
world, nevertheless, this year is William Blake's
The Mental Traveller set to sitar and gongs and
glockenspiel . . .

> For as he eats and drinks he grows
> Younger and younger every day;
> And on the desert wild they both
> Wander in terror and dismay . . .

The unvoiced fear represented by this song's sweeping of the world being that he may yet evade us; that he may slide down towards infancy, and at the moment of his birth (whatever life-support mechanisms extrude to keep him alive till then!) the VSTM will implode back whence it came: sick joke of some alien superconsciousness, intervening in human affairs with a scientific "miracle" to make all human striving meaningless and pointless. Not many people feel this way openly. It isn't a popular view. A man could be torn limb from limb for espousing it in public. The human mind will never accept it; and purges this fear in a long song of joy which at once mocks and copies and adores the mystery of the VSTM.

Men put this supreme man into the machine. Even so, Madonna and Child does haunt the world's mind. . . . and a soft femininity prevails—men's skirts are the new soft gracious mode of dress in the West. Yet he is now so noble, so handsome in his youth, so glowing and strong; such a Zarathustra, locked up in there.

(2018)

He can only be 21 or 22. The world adores him, mothers him, across the unbridgeable gulf of reversed time. No progress in the Solar System, let alone on the interstellar front. Why should we travel out and away, even as far as Mars, let alone Pluto, when a revelation is at hand; when all the secrets will be unlocked here on Earth? No progress on the tachyon or negative-time fronts, either. Nor any further messages from him. But he *is* his own message. His presence alone is sufficient to express Mankind: hopes, courage, holiness, determination.

(2019)
I am called back from retirement, for he is holding up signs again: the athlete holding up the Olympic Flame.

He holds them up for half an hour at a stretch— as though we are not all eyes agog, filming every moment in case we miss something, anything.

When I arrive, the signs that he has already held up have announced:

(Sign One) THIS IS A VERY SLOW TIME MACHINE. (And I amend accordingly, crossing out all the other titles we had bestowed on it successively, over the years. For a few seconds I wonder whether he was really naming the machine— defining it—or complaining about it! As though he'd been fooled into being its passenger on the assumption that a time machine should proceed to its destination *instanter* instead of at a snail's pace. But no. He was naming it.) TO TRAVEL INTO THE FUTURE, YOU MUST FIRST TRAVEL INTO THE PAST, ACCUMULATING HINDWARD POTENTIAL. (THIS IS CRAWLING DOWNHILL.)

(Sign Two) AS SOON AS YOU ACCUMULATE ONE

LARGE QUANTUM OF TIME, YOU LEAP FORWARD BY THE SAME TIMESPAN <u>AHEAD</u> OF YOUR STARTING POINT. (THIS IS SLIDING UPHILL.)

(Sign Three) YOUR JOURNEY INTO THE FUTURE TAKES THE SAME TIME AS IT WOULD TAKE TO LIVE THROUGH THE YEARS IN REAL-TIME; YET YOU ALSO <u>OMIT</u> THE INTERVENING YEARS, ARRIVING AHEAD INSTANTLY. (PRINCIPLE OF CONSERVATION OF TIME.)

(Sign Four) SO, TO LEAP THE GAP, YOU MUST CRAWL THE OTHER WAY.

(Sign Five) TIME DIVIDES INTO ELEMENTARY QUANTA. NO MEASURING ROD CAN BE SMALLER THAN THE INDIVISIBLE ELEMENTARY ELECTRON; THIS IS ONE "ELEMENTARY LENGTH" (EL). THE TIME TAKEN FOR LIGHT TO TRAVEL ONE EL IS "ELEMENTARY TIME" (ET): I.E., $10^{.23}$ SECONDS; THIS IS ONE ELEMENTARY QUANTUM OF TIME. TIME CONSTANTLY LEAPS AHEAD BY THESE TINY QUANTA FOR EVERY PARTICLE; BUT, NOT BEING SYNCHRONIZED, THESE FORM A CONTINUOUS TIME-OCEAN RATHER THAN SUCCESSIVE DISCRETE "MOMENTS" OR WE WOULD HAVE NO CONNECTED UNIVERSE.

(Sign Six) TIME REVERSAL OCCURS NORMALLY IN STRONG NUCLEAR INTERACTIONS I.E. IN EVENTS OF ORDER $10^{.23}$ SECS. THIS REPRESENTS THE "FROZEN GHOST" OF THE FIRST MOMENT OF UNIVERSE WHEN AN "ARROW OF TIME" WAS FIRST STOCHASTICALLY DETERMINED.

(Sign Seven) (And this is when I arrived, to be shown Polaroid photographs of the first seven signs. Remarkably, he is holding up each sign in a linear sequence from our point of view; a considerable feat of forethought and memory, though no less than we expect of him.) NOW IT IS INVARIABLE & FROZEN IN; YET UNIVERSE AGES. STRETCHING OF SPACE-TIME BY EXPANSION PROPAGATES "WAVES" IN THE SEA OF TIME, CARRYING TIME-ENERGY WITH PERIOD (X) PROPORTIONAL TO THE RATE OF EXPANSION, AND TO RATIO OF TIME ELAPSED TO TOTAL TIME AVAILABLE FOR THIS COSMOS FROM INITIAL CONSTRANTS. EQUATIONS FOR X YIELD A PERIOD OF 35 YEARS CURRENTLY AS ONE MOMENT OF MACRO-TIME WITHIN WHICH MACROSCOPIC TIME REVERSAL BECOMES POSSIBLE.

(Sign Eight) CONSTRUCT AN "ELECTRON SHELL" BY SYNCHRONIZING ELECTRON REVERSAL. THE LOCAL SYSTEM WILL THEN FORM A TIME-REVERSED MINI-COSMOS & PROCEED HINDWARDS TILL X ELAPSES WHEN TIME CONSERVATION OF THE TOTAL UNIVERSE WILL PULL THE MINI-COSMOS (OF THE VSTM) FORWARD INTO MESH WITH UNIVERSE AGAIN I.E. BY 35 PLUS 35 YEARS.

"But how?" we all cried. "How do you synchronize such an infinity of electrons? We haven't the slightest idea!"

Now at least we knew when he had set off: from 35 years after 1985. From next year. We are supposed to know all this by next year! Why has he waited so long to give us the proper clues?

And he is heading for the year 2055. What is there in the year 2055 that matters so much?

(Sign Nine) I DO NOT GIVE THIS INFORMATION TO YOU BECAUSE IT WILL LEAD TO YOUR INVENTING THE

VSTM. THE SITUATION IS QUITE OTHERWISE. TIME IS
PROBABILISTIC, AS SOME OF YOU MAY SUSPECT. I
REALIZE THAT I WILL PROBABLY PERVERT THE
COURSE OF HISTORY & SCIENCE BY MY ARRIVAL IN
YOUR PAST (MY MOMENT OF DEPARTURE FOR THE
FUTURE); IT IS IMPORTANT THAT YOU DO NOT KNOW
YOUR PREDICAMENT TOO EARLY, OR YOUR FRANTIC
EFFORTS TO AVOID IT WOULD GENERATE A TIME LINE
WHICH WOULD UNPREPARE YOU FOR MY SETTING
OFF. AND IT IS IMPORTANT THAT IT DOES ENDURE,
FOR I AM THE MATRIX OF MAN. I AM LEGION. I SHALL
CONTAIN MULTITUDES.

MY RETICENCE IS SOLELY TO KEEP THE WORLD ON
TOLERABLY STABLE TRACKS SO THAT I CAN TRAVEL
BACK ALONG THEM. I TELL YOU THIS OUT OF COM-
PASSION, AND TO PREPARE YOUR MINDS FOR THE AR-
RIVAL OF GOD ON EARTH.

"He's insane. He's been insane from the start."

"He's been isolated in there for some very good
reason. Contagious insanity, yes."

"Suppose that a madman could project his
madness—"

"He already has done that, for decades!"

"—no, I mean really project it, into the consciousness of the whole world; a madman with a
mind so strong that he acted as a template, yes a
matrix for everyone else, and made them all his
dummies, his copies; and only a few people
stayed immune who could build this VSTM to
isolate him—"

"But there isn't time to research it now!"

"What good would it do shucking off the problem for another thirty-five years? He would only
reappear—"

"Without his strength. Shorn. Senile. Broken. Starved of his connections with the human race. Dried up. A mental leech. Oh, he tried to conserve his strength. Sitting quietly. Reading, waiting. But he broke! Thank God for that. It was vital to the future that he went insane."

"Ridiculous! To enter the machine next year he must already be alive! He must already be out there in the world projecting this supposed madness of his. But he isn't. We're all separate sane individuals, all free to think what we want—"

"Are we? The whole world has been increasingly obsessed with him these last twenty years. Fashions, religions, life-styles: the whole world has been skewed by him ever since he was born! He must have been born about twenty years ago. Around 1995. Until then there was a lot of research into him. The tachyon hunt. All that. But he only began to obsess the world as a spiritual figure after that. From around 1995 or 6. When he was born as a baby. Only, we didn't focus our minds on his own infantile urges—because we had him here as an adult to obsess ourselves with—"

"Why should he have been born with infantile urges? If he's so unusual, why shouldn't he have been born already leeching on the world's mind; already knowing, already experiencing everything around him?"

"Yes, but the real charisma started then! All the emotional intoxication with him!"

"All the mothering. All the fear and adoration of his infancy. All the Bethlehem hysteria. Picking up as he grew and gained projective strength. We've been just as obsessed with Bethlehem as

with Nazareth, haven't we? The two have gone
hand in hand."

(Sign Ten) I AM GOD. AND I MUST SET YOU FREE. I
MUST CUT MYSELF OFF FROM MY PEOPLE; CAST MY-
SELF INTO THIS HELL OF ISOLATION.
   I CAME TOO SOON; YOU WERE NOT READY FOR ME.

   We begin to feel very cold; yet we cannot feel
cold. Something prevents us—a kind of malign
contagious tranquillity.
   It is all so right. It slots into our heads so exactly,
like the missing jigsaw piece for which the hole
lies cut and waiting, that we know what he said is
true; that he is growing up out there in our obsessed, blessed world, only waiting to come to us.

(Sign Eleven) (Even though the order of the signs
was time-reversed from his point of view, there
was the sense of a real dialogue now between him
and us, as though we were both synchronized. Yet
this wasn't because the past was inflexible, and he
was simply acting out a role he knew "from history". He was really as distant from us as ever. It
was the looming presence of himself in the real
world which cast its shadow on us, molded our
thoughts and fitted our questions to his re-
sponses; and we all realized this now, as though
scales fell from our eyes. We weren't guessing or
fishing in the dark any longer; we were being
dictated to by an overwhelming presence of
which we were all conscious—and which wasn't
locked up in the VSTM. The VSTM was Nazareth,

the setting-off point; yet the whole world was also Bethlehem, womb of the embryonic God, his babyhood, childhood and youth combined into one synchronous sequence by his all-know-ingness, with the accent on his wonderful birth that filtered through into human consciousness ever more saturatingly.) MY OTHER SELF HAS AC-CESS TO ALL THE SCIENTIFIC SPECULATIONS WHICH I HAVE GENERATED; AND ALREADY I HAVE THE SOLU-TION OF THE TIME EQUATIONS. I SHALL ARRIVE SOON & YOU SHALL BUILD MY VSTM & I SHALL ENTER IT; YOU SHALL BUILD IT INSIDE AN EXACT REPLICA OF THIS LABORATORY, SOUTHWEST SIDE. THERE IS SPACE THERE. (Indeed it had been planned to ex-tend the National Physical Laboratory that way, but the plans had never been taken up, because of the skewing of all our research which the VSTM had brought about.) WHEN I REACH MY TIME OF SET-TING OUT, WHEN TIME REVERSES, THE PROBABILITY OF THIS LABORATORY WILL VANISH, & THE OTHER WILL ALWAYS HAVE BEEN THE TRUE LABORATORY THAT I AM IN, INSIDE THIS VSTM. THE WASTE LAND WHERE YOU BUILD, WILL NOW BE HERE. YOU CAN WITNESS THE INVERSION: IT WILL BE MY FIRST PROB-ABILISTIC MIRACLE. THERE ARE HYPERDIMENSIONAL REASONS FOR THE PROBABILISTIC INVERSION, AT THE INSTANT OF TIME REVERSAL. BE WARNED NOT TO BE INSIDE THIS LABORATORY WHEN I SET OUT, WHEN I CHANGE TRACKS, FOR THIS SEGMENT OF REALITY HERE WILL ALSO CHANGE TRACKS, BECOMING IM-PROBABLE, SQUEEZED OUT.

(Sign Twelve) I WAS BORN TO INCORPORATE YOU IN

MY BOSOM; TO UNITE YOU IN A WORLD MIND, IN THE
PHASE SPACE OF GOD. THOUGH YOUR INDIVIDUAL
SOULS PERSIST, WITHIN THE FUSION. BUT YOU ARE
NOT READY. YOU MUST BECOME READY IN 35 YEARS'
TIME BY FOLLOWING THE MENTAL EXERCISES WHICH
I SHALL DELIVER TO YOU, MY MEDITATIONS. IF I RE-
MAINED WITH YOU NOW, AS I GAIN STRENGTH,
YOU WOULD LOSE YOUR SOULS. THEY WOULD BE
SUCKED INTO ME, INCOHERENTLY. BUT IF YOU GAIN
STRENGTH, I CAN INCORPORATE YOU COHERENTLY
WITHOUT LOSING YOU. I LOVE YOU ALL, YOU ARE
PRECIOUS TO ME, SO I EXILE MYSELF.

THEN I WILL COME AGAIN IN 2055. I SHALL RISE
FROM TIME, FROM THE USELESS HARROWING OF A
LIMBO WHICH HOLDS NO SOULS PRISONER, FOR YOU
ARE ALL HERE, ON EARTH.

That was the last sign. He sits reading again and
listening to taped music. He is radiant; glorious.
We yearn to fall upon him and be within him.

We hate and fear him too; but the Love washes
over the Hate, losing it a mile deep.

He is gathering strength outside somewhere: in
Wichita or Washington or Woodstock. He will
come in a few weeks to reveal himself to us. We all
know it now.

And then? Could we kill him? Our minds
would halt our hands. As it is, we know that the
sense of loss, the sheer bereavement of his departure hindwards into time will all but tear our souls
apart.

And yet . . . I WILL COME AGAIN IN 2055, he has
promised. And incorporate us, unite us, as separate thinking souls—if we follow all his medita-

tions; or else he will suck us into him as dummies, as robots if we do not prepare ourselves. What then, when God rises from the grave of time, in-sane?

Surely he knows that he will end his journey in madness! That he will incorporate us all, as conscious living beings, into the matrix of his own insanity?

It is a fact of history that he arrived in 1985 ragged, jibbering and lunatic—tortured beyond endurance by being deprived of us.

Yet he demanded, jubilantly, in 1997, confirmation of his safe arrival; jubilantly, and we lied to him and said YES! YES! And he must have believed us. (Was he already going mad from deprivation?)

If a laboratory building can rotate into the probability of that same building adjacent to itself: if time is probabilistic (which we can never prove or disprove concretely with any measuring rod, for we can never see *what has not been*, all the alternative possibilities, though they might have been), we have to wish what we know to be the truth, not to have been the truth. We can only have faith that there will be another probabilistic miracle, beyond the promised inversion of laboratories that he speaks of, and that he will indeed arrive back in 1985 calm, well-kept, radiantly sane, his mind composed. And what is this but an entrée into madness for rational beings such as us? We must perpetrate an act of madness; we must believe the world to be other than what it was—so that we can receive among us a Sane, Blessèd, Loving God in 2055. A fine preparation for the coming of a mad God! For if we drive ourselves mad, believing passionately what was not true, will we not infect him with our madness, so that he is/has to be/will be/and always was mad too?

Credo quia impossibilis; we have to believe because it is impossible. The alternative is hideous.

Soon. He will be coming. Soon. A few days, a few dozen hours. We all feel it. We are overwhelmed with bliss.

Then we must put him in a chamber, and lose Him, and drive Him mad with loss, in the sure and certain hope of a sane and loving resurrection thirty years hence—so that He does not harrow Hell, and carry it back to Earth with Him.

THY BLOOD LIKE MILK

This tale is for the sun god, Tezcatlipoca, with my curses, and for you Marina—whom I never knew enough to love—with apologies and blessings, somewhat tardy . . .

Have you ever screamed at your nurse to go away—to leave you in peace—and hated her, as bitterly as you've ever hated anybody? And begged her, as you never begged anyone in your proud life before?

Ten of us lay in the ward in the plastic webbing imprisoning us, yet only three of us really counted, Shanahan, Grocholski, and me, for we were the only presidents. Yet a big haul for them, indeed, three presidents! How cleverly the hospital distinguished between us and the ordinary runners: the extra dose of nerve sensitizer in the syringe, the absence of any opiates. We hung on the raw edge of pain, gritting our teeth as the taps were spun and at times—when our bloodstreams burned like second nervous systems on fire in our bodies, and it seemed like we were being roasted on a gridiron, from our insides outwards—at such times we let go and screamed. Whereas when the runners were being drained they moaned but did not need to scream. Mixed in with their quarter-pint soup of drugs (anti-shock, anti-coagulant, vitamins, iron) they received the opiates that let them still catch the idea of pain, but be somewhat glassed off from it—while we three were locked up in bright tin boxes with the howl of a thumbnail on slate a thousand times amplified. The nerve sensitizer wasn't merely sadistic, but meant to aid the nurse monitoring the effects of the milking on our bodies; the opiates were supposed to block off the worst of the sensations arising. I might say that according to the compensation laws we should have all had opiates. But that's how they ran a punishment ward. Idiot thinking. Shanahan, Grocholski, and I—we didn't hold each other's occasional screams and pleas against each other. The pain just happened to be unbearable. As simple as that. In the eyes of the runners our agony confirmed our presidencies. The Aztec priests were tortured by the Spaniards before their congregations. So the Aztec priests screamed and begged, when their turn came? Their congregations still believed in them.

"You scum of the earth!" Marina hissed as she jabbed our tethered buttocks with that cruel syringe, an Ahab tormenting her own private whale over and over again. (But I did not know her, did not know you as Marina yet.) "Do you know what will happen to you today? We're going to take so much out of you and for so long that your brain will starve for oxygen, you'll be half way to an idiot, a drooling vegetable."

"You know that's illegal, you bitch," I snarled as you tickled my bare flesh with the syringe anticipatorily making my nerves try to crawl away.

"Anyone may make mistakes," her eyes gleamed.

Only a scare, a put-on. Panic. She wouldn't dare.

"You must be a pretty girl under that mask. Why do you hate us so bitter?"

"Why give you the satisfaction of knowing?"

"You gave me the satisfaction of knowing just then—there's something to know."

And the syringe hit my flesh hard, at that, and dug in.

The hot acid gruel washed into me. My veins now lava-flows cursed with a consciousness of their own heat and motion. The exquisite agony of being emptied out. The pain of my tortured body racing to make more and more blood as the metabolic drugs goaded it on.

And under and around this pain, the fear that as life-blood flowed out through the taps, my brain was starving and impoverished, on the brink of becoming the brain of an animal, a toad, a stone—

"Bitch!" I screamed.

Out through one set of pipes flowed my rich blood, in through another the miserable substitute fluid that my body raced to build upon. And Marina (whom I did not know as Marina yet) danced the empty syringe before my eyes, to conduct the music of my torment—keeping an eye on the dials and gauges but pretending not to. Why did she hate us so bitter? Well, I hated her just as bitter! Why ask why. I knew it when I rode for the sun, I might end up here if they found one single excuse to lay their hands on me.

Then the pain got too bad to think about anything else.

No windows in the ward. What was there to look
out on? We were outside any Fuller dome, in this
hospital. The pollution crawling up and down the
sides of the building, dark grey to pitch black. A
general turbidity over the land: over the great
plains where the braves of another age and world
hunted buffalo; on the treeless hills, where it had
long since snuffed out the pines; pressing soft on
the Great Dead Lakes, and, further out, pressing
soft on the dark cesspool of the North Atlantic.
Pressing upon the superhighways where mostly
automatic traffic crawled and where we had
hunted in our packs for that rare bird of paradise,
that dark orchid, the patch of clear sun—the
"sunspot" that blooms mysteriously amid the
murk, shafts of gold piercing a funnel of light
down to earth whereby the clear sky could be
briefly glimpsed and worshipped. Were not the
deaths we caused on the highways only petty
sacrifices to ensure the coming of the sun?

And the murk lay thickly on this hospital,
Superhighway 31 Crash Hospital, Prison Wing, in
whose ward we swooned in pain as we gave up
our lifeblood to recompense the beneficiaries of
this murk, authors of the forever eclipse of the
sun . . .

When did I set out upon the sun trail? When did I
drive down my own superhighway of the spirit,
choosing my own side of the split world, the zone
of blood and the sun? Oh these years of hunting
for the sun—down ten times a thousand miles of
gloomy darkness, oily globules crawling on our
windshields, eyes glazed by the green gleaming

radar screens of our sun buggies as we swung them, steering blind, through the rivers of automated slave cars, slave trucks riding their guide lines! Brains blazing with the data stream from Meteorology Central—the temperature gradients, the shifting chemistry of the pollutants, the swirling shapes of air turbidity, the cat's cradle of contrails spied upon by the satellite stations high above! (Have you seen a picture of the Earth from satellite? The masked globe, in its gossamer spidery web of contrails, a mud of many shades of brown ochre grey stirred slowly, punctured in several magic shifting locations by the white walls of sunspots drilling their way to the barren ground or the dead seas or the great photophobic anaerobic algae beds (where, perversely, the light kills them) or the dots of Fuller domes where the wasp world lives out its memories of middle class existence.) Grabbing the data with our minds to make a gestalt of it that will lead us to the sun! These years of hunting for the sun—and finding it! Being first to reach those clear fresh zones of radiance, where the flash harvests green and bronze the earth, and tiny flowers rage and seed and die within the span of thirty minutes. Being the only men to see it. To know that nature was still fleetingly alive, in an accelerated abbreviated panic form, still mistress of a panic beauty. These years of discovering the sun and duelling for it on the highways, and ever in the back of our minds somewhere awareness of the Compensation Laws—the blood-debt to be settled.

"Hey," called Shanahan, as Marina came to him

next in line with the syringe primed and loaded, a
little bit of machismo on his part. "Why not come
for a ride in my sun buggy after I get out of here?
I'll drive you into the deep dark countryside and
we won't hunt for no sunspots either. What we've
got to do, we can do in the dark! Hey—but come to
think of it—why not just come on a sun hunt with
me? Put a blush of real genuine sunburn on those
delicate while limbs of yours. Or could it be that
you're just a wasp that buzzes about a sundome
for her holidays, and never flies out?"

"Yes I'm a wasp, this is my sting."

And she stung Shanahan's quivering buttocks
with the syringe, putting an abrupt end to his
taunts. He hung in the white plastic webbing,
twitching with pain, fat fly in a spider's web that
he couldn't break out of. Marina spun the taps,
spiderlike sucked him dry, until he howled.

Till he screamed like ice, like thumbnails on
slate.

And Marina—with what grim delight you
watched him writhing.

With as much magic and mysticism in the hunt
for the sun as there was meteorology, remember
how we met together to plot strategies, when our
own sun club—Smoking Mirror—first coalesced
(later to be known as Considine's Commandos)?
And the Indian runner, Marti, who said that his
great great granddaddy had been an Indian magician, who stayed with Smoking Mirror till one
black afternoon he pushed his buggy too fast, too
wildly for a mere machine, down a highway
crowded with slave traffic, perceptions throbbing

with input, idea associations swarming, sense of time and space distraught—for he'd taken a peyotl pill to commune with his magical ancestry. Marti, who knew all the sun myths of all the Indians, South and North, of the Americas. Marti, who said the name we should call ourselves by—Smoking Mirror—alias of the savage wealthy treacherous Aztec sun god, Tezcatlipoca. Marti, who wore the obsidian knife round his neck on a leather thong. The same knife (stolen from a museum case) that the Aztec priests used to tear out the palpitating hearts of the prisoners sacrificed to Tezcatlipoca.

When we reached his smashed buggy and went out to it in our oxygen masks (we had a few minutes before the patrols arrived from the nearest emergency point, with their Compensation Laws to enforce on us, for the flanks of the highway were strewn with the wreckage of the slave cars Marti had collided with) we found the obsidian knife had turned, by a freak, as Marti struck the steering wheel, and driven itself into his chest.

I pulled it out and hung it in my buggy and never washed the blood off the blade. We met the sun that day, the next day, and for three days after—blazing sun spots drilling their way through the smog as we charted our crazy sad, angry course of mourning and celebration of Marti's spirit, across the continent, till even Meteorology Central sat up and took notice of the wild unstatistical improbability of our successes (a first sighting of a sunspot is a kind of scalp, see? a new brave's feather in our headdress) and the sun hordes came tracking us from all over the land to batten on us, converging, duelling, crashing towards us, driving our luck away—Tezcatlipoca would only reveal himself to us, to praise Marti who had named us in his honor.

Only after that when Marti had become history (though the dark-stained knife still hung in my buggy) the new name Considine's Commandos became known, and we settled down to a long period of reasonable successes, but never so successful as that one wild week after Marti died, sacrificed to the sun.

We duelled on the highways with the other clubs, skittering through the slave convoys where the wasps sat back in waspish disbelief with their windows blanked, lapping up video reruns and playing Scrabble, hearing occasionally the scream of tires from the impossible Outside, brief nightmare intrusion on their security, banshees, werewolfs, spooks haunting the wide open Darks between the Fuller domes.

One club that even called themselves the Banshees we tangled with on the southern highways, knowing them only by their radar blips, sneers and taunts over the radio, till one day—or night, where's the difference?—we all of us happened into the same bar at the same time, and I was carrying Marti's obsidian knife, beneath my shirt, or I would never have walked out of that bar to drive again. This time Marti had saved me, but the knife had other enemy blood on it now; and Marti's spirit seemed to disappear. At the cost of losing us the sun, he saved me. For weeks we hunted. For months. And nothing. We got to loathe the midnight roundup of the sunspot sightings from Met Central. Things were beginning to fall apart.

Would have done, maybe, if we hadn't been cracked wide open, by the day that brought the Compensation Laws down on all our heads.

"You know what I'd do to that bitch if we were out of these plastic cocoons," Grocholski growled. "That bitch" was around the corner preparing our meals. "I'd rip off her sweet white mask and sweet white uniform, hook her up to this marvel of medical science and drain her whole damn bloodstream while I raped her as cool and clinical as you like, and put no liquid back in her but my seed—what's one fluid ounce to eight pints of the red stuff?—and I'd leave her hanging here in the web for her friends to find like veal in a slaughterhouse."

Vicious sentiments, Grocholski. But Grocholski had performed just as nasty as that—as cool and clinical, I had heard, though I hadn't met the man before the hospital threw us together here in the ward. He had pulled a girl's teeth out with pliers, one by one, for trying to walk out on him . . .

Vicious enough to bring Marina out, so genuinely distraught that she ripped off her white gauze mask and let us take a look at her full face for the first time—beautiful, I thought, amazed, though I hardly dared let myself admit it—not Barbi-dolly or Bambi-cute, but strong with a warp somewhere in it, maybe in the twist of the lips, that gave her the stamp of authenticity—being unlike the million other stereotypes from the same mold. And her green eyes blazed, till they boiled with tears that evaporated almost as she shed them, so hotly angry was she.

"I don't believe in any heaven. For you vicious

beasts killed my man. My heaven was here on
Earth! But now I believe in hell. And I know how
to make a hell for you. Nobody will get any opiates
from now on. Nobody. Thanks to your polite-
ness."

"Hey," protested a runner from his white webbing. "You don't have the right to deprive us—
that's illegal!"

"Isn't your people's philosophy outside the
Law?"

I tried to tell her then, because suddenly I
wanted her to know.

"We do have a code to follow, the same as
you—it's a different code, is all . . ."

You didn't hear me, Marina, or you didn't seem
to. For Shanahan was shouting:

"They always used the Indian women as torturers! The girls made the best!"

So he'd noticed, too, how high your cheek
bones were, though masked and hidden partly by
your rounded cheeks, the skin not pulled so
tight—sealskin over a canoe frame—the way it
had been with some Indian girls I'd known, riding
for the sun with us, recognizing—and that was
what I wanted you to understand, Marina—how
we were the new buffalo hunters of the darkness,
the new braves and warriors of the polluted
darkened highways.

Then things got noisy in the ward. The act of
freeing your mouth from the mask's embrace had
freed all of our mouths too—but not so much for
taunts and obscenities, for a while, till it turned
ugly again, but for pointed remarks directed at a
real and sexy—if hostile—woman.

With the mask off you became more real, and though we still hated you, we couldn't dismiss you as a perfect plastic wasp girl anymore. At least I couldn't. You'd graduated to the status of an enemy.

Marina stared round the ward hotly, at the devils hanging in hell in their plastic wrappings, waiting helplessly to repay their debts to society—and made no move to put her mask back on.

She even answered a question.

"Why do I do this? I volunteered. It's not a popular job, dealing with your people. I volunteered, so I could hurt some of you the way that I've been hurt."

"How have you been hurt, Princess?" yawned Grocholski.

"Didn't you hear her saying we'd killed her man, Gr'olski?"

You gazed at me bitterly, yet in your unmasked gaze was a kind of salutation.

"How did it happen?"

"How do you think you kill good men? You ran him down in the dark, deliberately, while he was tending at an accident."

"Did you see it yourself?"

"Wasps can't see to fly in the dark," jeered Grocholski, carrying machismo further into the zone of his own personal viciousness.

"That's how I know," Marina told me icily, ignoring Grocholski, who was thrashing about in his web simulating laughter. "Talk like that. Attitudes like that. Oh, he could see you coming on the radar screen before he stepped out of the ambulance. He could see. But he stayed out on the

road to rescue a woman caught in a burning car.
He was still foaming it down when you ran him
over. You dragged him half a mile. They wouldn't
let me see him, he was so smashed."

"Wouldn't *let* you see him?" Grocholski caught
out of what she said—but he didn't press the
point.

And I wanted her to know—to really understand, inside herself—what we people had, when
we weren't being vicious beasts—how we were
the real authentic people of our times, facing up to
the dirt and dark outside instead of hiding in
Fuller domes, hunting down the last glimpses of
the natural world—the sun, the sky! How we were
the last braves, the last hunters—how could I get
that through to the Indian in you smothered in the
plastic waspish flesh?

"The ambulance man saw it all on radar—how
you changed course at the last moment, to hit him,
out there on the road."

"Ambulance man probably hated us anyway—
tell any sort of lie."

"Do you," in that frozen voice that I yearned to
melt, "deny you run men down just for kicks?"

"You're not so kind yourself, are you? Why not
ask yourself deep down what you're doing here
torturing us—whether you aren't enjoying it? Revenge? A long revenge, hey! Something you're
specializing in?" (Dared I say it yet—and expect
you to accept at least a little bit of it—if not immediately, then later maybe when you were
alone, lying awake in bed and worried because
something had gone astray in your scheme of
things?) "You're interested in us beasts. You took

this job to be near us. Like a zoo visitor watches the tigers. Smell our musk, our fear, our reality."

Marina's hand cracked across my face, so hard my whole body rocked in its white cocoon.

I swallowed the taste of blood in my mouth and stared hard at her, whispered:

"True, it's true, think about it."

A look of horror came into her eyes, as she quickly pulled the gauze mask over nose and mouth again.

I suppose the Compensation Laws worked our way too. How else could it be, in a split society?

They bought our tacit support for the maintenance of "civilized" life—the deceits that otherwise we'd have done our best to explode, us sunclubbers, saboteurs, ghettopeople, all of us outlaws (whom it's plain ridiculous to call outlaw when full fifty per cent of the people live outside of wasp society). And the wasp world could only blast us out of existence by turning its own massive nuclear artillery upon itself—so, in return for the relative security of its slave superhighways, our own relative freedom to roam them. If the wasp world put too many feet wrong, explosives would go off in its highway tunnels, gatherings of the tribes pull down a Fuller dome, a satellite shuttle plane blasting off be met by a home-made missile with a home-made warhead on it. And if we put too many feet wrong (taking wasp lives with our sun buggies was one way) and if they caught us, there would be a blood debt to pay, hooked up to their milking machines, where we were not supposed to be hurt too much, or die, or

get brain damage, but just *repay, repay* society.
For they need red blood like vampires need it.

So I began working on your mind, Marina.

As for the others, well, Grocholski's thoughts
were of tearing his enemies' teeth out with pin-
cers, he knew nothing about minds. A king—but a
stupid king, like many kings who must have
triumphed over the stupidity of their subjects by a
greater and crueller stupidity.

Shanahan was a subtler sort of president, had
some idea what we stood for, could put it some
way into words. Yet he couldn't see his way clear,
as I could, into this woman's soul with all its
possibilities.

And you worked on my body, Marina.

Neglected your promised cruelties to the
others. Still treated Shanahan and Grocholski like
dirt, but carelessly, indifferently, reserving your
finest moments for me.

And I tried to grit my teeth through the pain and
not scream out meaningless noises or empty
curses, but always something that would drill the
hole deeper and deeper into you—as the sun drills
through the smog—till the protective layers were
undercut and the egg of myself could be laid in
your heart.

"Milkmaid with buckets of blood in your yoke,
why not believe me?" I winced, as Marina thrust
the gruel of drugs into the tender parts of my
body. "We're hunting for something real in a dirty
world—the dirt you wasps have spread around,
till there's such a pile you have to hide yourselves
away from it."

She drained the blood from me till I fainted, green eyes boring into me, doting on my pain. . . .

The Myth of the Five Suns—how brightly Marti told it one day after a long fruitless race for the sun that took us near five hundred miles across the plains, till we pulled in tired and restless at a service area run by ghettopeople with their hair like head-dresses, like black coronas around eclipsed suns.

"Five worlds there were," said Marti, the pupils of his eyes dilated to black marbles, his tight brown skin over small sharp bones like a rabbit sucked dry by ants, wizened by the desert sunshine that he had smarted under in his dreams. "In the first World men swam about like fishes under a Sun of Jewels. This world perished in a flamestorm brought about by the rising of the second sun, the Sun of Fire. The fishes changed into chickens and dogs that raced about in the great heat, unwilling to pause for their feet were burning. But this Sun of Fire died down in turn, gave way to the Sun of Darkness, whose people fed upon pitch and resin. They in their turn were swallowed up by an earthquake and a Sun of Wind arose. The few survivors of the Sun of Darkness became hairy dancing monkeys that lived on fruit. But the fifth sun was the Sun of Light— the one the ancient Mexicans knew. Which sun are we under now, can you riddle me that?"

"Sun of Darkness," answered one of the ghettopeople. "Here's your pitch and resin to eat." Dumping our plates of hamburgers, which may have been made from oil sludge or algae—so perhaps he was right in a way.

Then Snowflake—of the snub nose and blond pigtails, with her worry beads of rock-hard dried chestnuts on a silver chain—who was riding with Marco in his buggy—wanted to tell a story herself, and Marti let her go ahead while we were consuming the burgers.

"There was this waspman, see, whose slave car broke down on the highway miles from town, and quite by chance in the midst of a sunspot. He'd lost all sense of time on the journey, watching video, so when the car stopped he thought he'd reached his destination—especially when he opened the car door and saw the sun shining and a blue sky overhead, like at home in the Fuller dome. He got out of the car, too busy with his briefcase to notice that under that sun and that blue sky the land stretched out black and devastated, a couple inches deep in sludge. An area where some light-hating plants had taken over, see, which had the trick of dissolving if the sun came out . . ."

"What?" cried Marco, indignant.

"Shut up, this is a story! At that moment the power came on in his car again and away it whisked, leaving him standing there on the road. Other cars zipped by on either side. He waved his arms at them and held his briefcase up but all the passengers were watching video and had their windows opaqued. He got scared and leapt off the road into the sludge. However the sunspot was coming to a close now. The blue sky misted over and soon he was all alone in the darkness with cars zipping by on one side and a hand clutching down his throat for his lungs as the pollution flowed back, his eyes watering onion tears. And in the darkness, doubly blinded by tears, he wandered further and further away from the road into the sludge. Even the noise of the cars seemed to be coming four ways at once to him. But now it was dark again the sludge was coming together, shaping itself into fungi two feet high, and amoeba things as big as his foot, and wet mucous tendrils like snots ten feet long that coiled and writhed about . . . and all kinds of nameless nightmares were there in the darkness squelching and slobbering about him . . . So he went mad, I guess. Or maybe he was mad to start with."

A few runners, a few of the ghettopeople applauded, but Marco looked disgusted at her butting in—though our mouths had been full while she was doing the talking—and Marti expressed his annoyance at what he thought of as her sloppy nursery horror-comic world, preferring his horror neat like raw spirit, and religious and classical—and as we drank off our tart metallic beer (solution of iron filings) to wash the burgers down, he dwelt on the how and when of the Aztec sacrifices to the sun.

"Oh handsome was the prisoner they taught to play the flute and smoke in a neat and elegant fashion and sing like Caruso. After a year of smoking and singing and playing the flute, four virgins were given to him to make love to. Ten days after that they took him out onto the last terrace of the temple. They opened his chest with one single slash of a knife. This knife." (He whirled the obsidian blade on the thong from around his neck, where he'd hung it when he left the buggy, flashed it at us.) "Unzipped him, tore out his heart!"

How strange, and remarkable, that the heartblood of the Aztecs' prisoner flowing for the sun should become our own heartblood pumped into storage bottles and refrigerated with glycerol at this hospital! A sacrifice of ice against a sacrifice of fire—both harshly painful—the one lasting as long as an iceberg melting, the other over and done with in a flash of time!

Waking up weak-headed but set in my purpose, growing sharper with each hour, I shouted for you to come to my web-side, as Shanahan and Grocholski stared at me bemused and grumbled to one another about this perversion of machismo.

"Nurse!"

And you drifted to my side, green eyes agleam, hate crystals in your Indian skull.

"What is it, Considine?"

"Mightn't you hurt me a bit more if I knew you were a person with a name? A nameless torturer never had much fun. Wouldn't you love to be begged for mercy by name—the way he called you by name, with emotion—the emotions of fear and anguish, if not of love? The victim begs to know his tormentor's name."

"So you're a victim, are you?"

"We're all victims of this dirty world."

"No, you're not victims, not you people. You're here to pay because you made victims of other people. So that the lives of your future victims may be saved, by your own life-blood."

Almost as an afterthought, you added softly:
"My name's Marina, Considine."
"Ah."
Then I could let my forced attention unfocus
and disperse into the foggy wool of fading
pain . . .

And when she came again to plunge the bitter
drugs into my body and spin the taps that recom-
menced the sacrifice of blood, she murmured,
eyes agleam with the taunting of me:
"Your blood has saved two lives already,
Considine—that must please you."
"Marina," I hissed before she had a chance to
stick the syringe in me, "Marina, it's only a role in
our game that you're playing, don't you realize?
In our Sunhunter's game! For sure it's our game,
ours, not yours!"
She held the syringe back, letting me see the
cruel needle.
"You know the name of the game, Marina? No,
of course you don't, in your white sterile uniform
and your plastic waspish life, how could you ever
know? But if you've really got Indian blood in
your veins, that might help you understand . . ."
"What's there to understand, Considine? I see
nothing to understand except you're scared of a
little pain."
"Not scared," I lied. "The pain, the savagery—
has to be. You have to hurt me, it's your destiny.
Day by day you sacrifice me to the sun, my priestess!"
While she still hung back from me, listening
in spite of herself, I told her something of
Tezcatlipoca—of the giant in an ashen veil carry-

ing his head in his hand, of the pouncing jaguar, of the dreadful shadow, of the bear with brilliant eyes. Of how he brought riches and death. Of the blood sacrifices on the last terrace of the temple. I told how Marti's knife had turned against his own bosom and how the sun had greeted us in splendor every day for a week thereafter. She went on listening, puzzled and angry, till the anger overcame the puzzlement in her, and she thrust the syringe home . . .

But of Tezcatlipoca the trickster I hadn't told her—nor of his deadly practical jokes.

How he arrived at a festival and sang a song (the song the prisoners were taught to sing) so entrancing that all the villagers followed him out of town, where he lured them onto a flimsy bridge, which collapsed, tossing hundreds of them down into the rocky gorge. How he walked into a village with a magic puppet dancing in his hand (the dance the prisoners were taught to dance) that lured the villagers closer and closer in their dumb amazement, till scores of them suffocated in the crush. How he pretended to be sorry, told the angry survivors that he couldn't guarantee his conduct, that they had better stone him to death to prevent more innocent victims succumbing to his tricks. And stone him to death they did. But his body stank so vilely, that many more people sickened and died before they could dispose of it.

As I lay there wracked with pain, these stories spun through my head in vivid bloodstained pictures, and my mind sang the song that led the sun's victims onto the bridge, and my body danced the twitching dance that suffocated the survivors, and my sweat glands and my excrement stank them to death.

How would I, Considine, sun's Messenger, lead and dance and stink Marina out of this bright-lit ward, into the darkness that was my home?

When a doctor made his rounds of the blood dairy, he remarked how roughly I was being treated.

"Don't kill the goose that lays the golden egg!" he twinkled, to Marina. No doubt nurses had broken down on this hateful job before.

I smiled at her when he said that, for after a time assuredly the victim and the torturer became accomplices, and when that happens their roles are fast becoming interchangeable. I grinned the death-grin of Tezcatlipoca as he lay dead in the village and stank the villagers into vulture fodder for a joke. . . .

So the Doctor thought she might try to assassinate me, snuff me out! Surely the least likely outcome of our duel, by now.

The sacrifice was always preceded by a period of great sensual indulgence—a recompense for the pain to be suffered. Yet this victim here, myself, was tied down, bound in white plastic thongs, while his tormentor hung over him day by day replaying a feeble mimic spearthrust into his body, spilling his blood but replacing it again. Day by day it hurt rackingly, yet death never came. What could come? Only freedom—reversal of the sacrifice—overwhelming pleasure—triumph—and the sun! My pain-wracked grin glowed confident, drove wild anguished discords through Marina's heart.

"Be careful, Nurse—this one's metabolic rate is far too high. He's burning himself up."

"Yes, yes," murmured Marina, distractedly, fleeing from me across the dark plateaux of her heart. . . .

And, when more days had passed and I felt invincible in my agony, I commanded:

"Come to me, Marina."

Does the male spider command the female spider to come to him with her ruthless jaws? Does the male mantis command the female mantis who will wrench his head off with her sawblade elbows?

"Marina."

She came to my side, under the bemused gaze of Shanahan and Grocholski, who had given up trying to understand, and, unblessed by the presence of Tezcatlipoca in their skulls, were glad enough to lie back in their plastic webs relaxing from those first few days of machismo, happy enough that the heat was off them. They kept quiet and watched me wonderingly as I suffered and commanded.

"Marina."

"Yes, Considine?"

"The time's approaching, Marina."

"Time, Considine?"

"There has to be a climax. What climax can there be? Think!"

"I . . ."

"I'll make it easier for you. You can't drain me dry. Can't . . . terminate me. What satisfaction would there be in that? Who would you turn to then? To Shanahan? Grocholski? Look at them.

Lying like slugs in their beds—great torpid bullies. What satisfaction would there be? Sure, Grocholski is a bastard, he'd pull your teeth out one by one with a pair of pliers. But has he any . . . spirit? Has the sun god whispered in his ear?"

Marina turned, watching the two presidents lolling in their white webs, shook her head—as though she understood the question.

Turning, she whispered:

"What climax, Considine?"

"I'll tell you tomorrow Marina—unless you can tell me before then. Sleep on it Marina, sleep on it . . ."

She came to me in the night like a sleepwalker—Lady with a Pencil Torch, whose beam she played over the webbing till she located the release tag, and there she rested her hand but didn't pull it yet-a-while.

As she knelt there bereft of her mask, her face level with mine, I gazed at her, not as avenging fury and priestess, but briefly as another human being passing in the dark. She knelt poised at the mid-point of a transformation in her role, for a brief time quietly happy in the lightening of the burden, the falling away of the robe of one office before the assumption of the next.

This pause must have lasted you an eternity, Marina.

I watched the long high planes of your cheeks in the backwash of light off the plastic webbing, the hilltops of your cheekbones, sharper now in the contrast of dark and bright—and your eyes

dark pools beyond the cheekbones, in shadow—
and kept my peace.

Tezcatlipoca took the form of an ashen-veiled
giant carrying his head in his hand and searched
for the sunspot where he could be himself, the
sun. The sight of him in the dark made nervous
people fall dead with fear, the way the wasps in
their slave cars shivered at our banshee wail as we
passed them by on the highways, invisible, vin-
dictive, reckless. Yet one brave man seized hold of
the giant and held on to him—bound him in white
plastic webbing, in spite of his screams and
curses. Held him hour after hour till near morning
when it was time for the sun to rise. Then the
ashen giant began promising the brave man
wealth and even omnipotence to let him go. At the
promise of omnipotence the brave man agreed
and tore out the giant's heart as a pledge before he
let him go. Wrapping the heart up in his handkerchief, he took it home with him. When he opened
it up to look at the heart, however, there was
nothing but ashes in it. For the sun had already
risen, and in his new omnipotence broke his
promise and burned his pledge.

Take heed, Marina, hand on the release tag—
take heed of the sun when he is free. You hold my
heart now in your handkerchief, blood drips into
your bottles through the mesh, safely. The heart is
not yet ashes.

Her hand touching the webbing, her Indian face
divided by a watershed of light . . . at this brief
pause in time could I have afforded a little pity, a
little affection . . . ?

"Is it time . . . ?"

She whispered into the darkness from which the sun must rise—for the sun is time itself (or so I thought then) so far as our twenty-four hour clocks knew, so far as the circadian rhythms of our bodies are aware.

What else is time, but the sun in the sky? But this is the Age Without Time—for the travellers over the blackened prairies, for the wasp refugees in the Fuller domes!

At the end of every fifty-two years, the fires were all quenched throughout Mexico, and a fresh fire kindled on a living prisoner's chest—to keep time on the move. What fire shall be kindled in whose chest, to bring Time back into the world today?

"Yes, it's time to kindle the sun."

Marina's breast rose and fell convulsively as she pulled the tag.

Plastic thongs slid off my limbs in four directions at once like frightened snakes and I slipped to the floor, free of the pain hammock, knocking aside the sanitary facilities which she'd forgotten to remove, with a noisy clatter that alerted Shanahan. He craned his head against the tension of the web, as I sat massaging life into my limbs.

"Considine," he called softly. A worried Marina flashed the pencil of light across his face, and he blinked blindly at us.

"Considine, get me out of here—please!"

"Put him back to sleep, Marina." (Quietly.) "It's not his time for release—Tezcatlipoca isn't with him." My feet prickling intolerably with thawing-out frostbite.

She crept towards Shanahan, dazzling him

with her pencil of light; injected him with something, while he imagined his web was being un-
done. By the time my legs were fit to stand on, he
was calm again.

She gripped my arm to steady me, helped me
dress.

"Your car's in the ambulance sheds."

"Buggy," said I angrily. "Sun buggy."

"There's so much I have to learn."

"There isn't much," I assured her—and this,
alas, was honest—as we slipped out of the ward
toward the darkness of freedom.

"What is the sun really like?"

"A ball of incandescent gas . . ."

Of course Marina hadn't seen the sun. Except
as a baby, long time ago, forgotten, maybe. Models
of the sun were all. Hot yellow lamps hanging
from the eggshells of the Fuller domes, switched
on in the morning, switched off again at night. If
a sunspot had ever bathed the hospital, she
wouldn't have seen it through the solid walls.

As we crept into the ambulance sheds, she
began to cough, grating explosive little coughs
that she did her best to stifle with her hand.

A dull orange glow from standby lighting per-
vaded the gloom of the sheds, where half a dozen
of the great sleek snub-nosed ambulances were
parked and a number of impounded buggies—
beyond, light spilling from a window in the crew
room door and the sound of muffled voices.

We climbed into my buggy—the key was in the
lock—and I ran my hands gently over the controls, reuniting myself with them.

Tezcatlipoca's jaguar stenciled on my seat radiated confidence strength suppleness and savagery through my body. . . .

Marina sat limply in the passenger seat looking around my world, stifling her cough—but the air was cleaner in my buggy, would get even cleaner once we were on the move.

"Who opens the doors?"

"We have to wait for an ambulance to leave, then chase it out. How soon till we see the sun, Considine?"

"Sooner than you think."

"How do you *know*?"

"What is the sun, Marina? A blazing yellow ball of gas radiating timelessly and forever at six thousand degrees Centigrade, too bright to look upon. A bear with bells on his ankles, striped face, blazing eyes. A magician with a puppet dancing in his hand. A smoking mirror. A giant in an ashen veil with his head in his hand. A G-type star out on the edge of the galaxy around which planets and other debris revolve. Your choice."

"I've seen movies of the sun—maybe it's no big thing after all."

"Oh it's big, Marina—it's the climax."

Then a siren went off in the shed, shockingly loud, and the lights came up full.

The ambulance crew spilled from their room, zipping their gear and fixing their masks as they ran. They took an ambulance two along the line from us.

Its monobeam flared out ahead, splashing a hole bright as the sun's disc on the door. Its turbines roared.

And the door flowed smoothly, swiftly, up into the roof.

As I started the buggy's engine a look of fear and terrible understanding came over Marina's face—sleepwalker wakening on the high cliff edge. She tore at the door handle. But naturally it was locked and she couldn't tell where to unlock it.

"Marina!" Using the voice that cuts through flesh to the bone. "Quit it!" A voice I'd never used to beg or plead with in the hospital. Authority voice of the Sun Priest. Obsidian voice. Voice that cuts flesh. Black, volcanic, harsh.

Her hand fell back upon the seat.

The ambulance, blinding the smog with its monobeam, sped through the doors—and us after it, before the doors dropped again.

Great Tezcatlipoca, Who Bringeth Wealth and War, Sunshine and Death, Sterility and Harvest! For Whom Blood Floweth Like Milk, That Milk May Flow!

The smog so thick outside. Even the great eye of the ambulance saw little. Undoubtedly they were relying on radar already, as I was—and wondering, doubtless, what the tiny blip behind their great blip represented, Remora riding on a shark . . . I dropped back, not to worry them.

When we got to the highway entry point, I took the other direction.

Whichever way I took, I knew it led to the sun.

Two hours down the highway, Marina sleeping on my shoulder, bored with the monotonous environment of the sun buggy (green radar no substitute for video), radio crackling out data from

Met Central revealing total disarray among the air currents, turbid gas blowing everywhichways, absurd peaks and dips in the nitrogen oxides, crazy chemical transformations—a scene in disarray awaiting my touch, and what I brought it was the body of Marina, magnet to the iron filings of the everywhichways polluted sky.

Two hours down the highway, piloting with ever-greater certainty, careless of pursuit, I picked the radiophone up, tuned to the Sun Club waveband. . . .

Nearby, voices of some charioteers of the sun.

"Considine calling you. Considine's Commandos. Smokey Mirror Sun Club. I'm heading straight for the sun. Anyone caring to join me is welcome. Vector in on my call sign . . ."

My voice woke Marina up, to the babble of voices answering over the radiophone.

"Considine?"

"How did you get out?"

"How do you *know*? Man?"

Who had ever dared call a hunt into being among sunrunners other than his own? How great the risk he ran, of shame, revenge, contempt!

How did I know, indeed!

"Where are we?" yawned Marina. "What's going on?"

"We're hunting for the sun—I've cried fox and I'm calling the hounds in."

"Whose voices are those?"

"It hasn't been done before, what I'm doing. Those voices—the cry of the hounds."

"Considine, I'm hungry. Is there anything to eat in the car?"

"Hush—I've told you, buggy is the name. No

eating now—it's time to fast. This is a religious moment."

A louder challenging voice that I recognized broke in on the waveband. The Magnificent Amberson's.

"Considine? This is Amberson. Congratulations on your break-out—how did you do it?"

"Thanks, Amberson. I got a nurse to spring me."

"A nurse?"

"She's with me now—she's part of it."

"Hope you know what you're doing, Considine. You really meaning to call a general hunt?"

"A gathering of the tribes. That's it, Amberson."

"Sure your head isn't screwed up by loss of blood? The weather data is chaos. Sure you haven't bought your way out of there by offering something in return—say, a gathering of the tribes in a certain location?"

"Screw you, Amberson—I'll settle with you for that slander after I've greeted the sun. Sun hounds, you coming chasing me?"

And a rabble of voices, from far and near, jammed the waveband.

Marina clutched my arm.

"It frightens me, Considine—who are they all? Where do they come from?"

"Some of the other half of the people in this land, Marina—just some of the other half of the people. The ones who stayed outside in the dark. The ones that weren't wasps. The Indians your ancestors would have understood. Spirit voices they are—gods of the land."

"Indians my ancestors?"

"Yes."

Green blips swam by me on the radar screen—slave cars that I sped by effortlessly. I paid no heed to the weather data. My gestalt, my mind-doll, was fully formed. Its embodiment hunched by me in the passenger seat, the curves and planes of Marina's body were the fronts and isobars and isohets of the surrounding dirt-darkened land. A message, she had been placed in the hospital for me to find, with pain the trigger to waken me to her meaning. So many forms a true message can take—a circle of giant stones of the megalith builders, a bunch of knotted strings of different lengths and colours (the quipu archives of the Incas)—a human body if need be. If the human body becomes a world unto the lover or the torturer, may not the world itself with its dales and hillocks, its caves and coverts and cliffs, be a body? Marina, my chart, on whom I read my destination!

"Now you must take your clothes off, Marina, for you'll soon be bathing in the sun—we'll soon be lovers."

"My clothes?"

"Do so."

I used the Voice of the Sun, the Voice from the Sky. And dazed she began to fumble at her nurse's uniform.

Her nudity clarified my mind—I knew exactly where to turn off now, on to which decrepit smaller road.

"Sun hounds!" I sang. "Don't miss the turning."

Goosebumps marched across Marina's flesh and her nipples stood out in the mental cold of her life's climax—the dawning awareness that she had been inserted into life long ago and grown into precisely this, and this, shape, as hidden marker for the greatest future sunspot, burning spot of all burning spots that might start the clouds of darkness rolling back across the land at last, burning away the poisoned blackened soup from the Earth's bowl in a flame-oven of renewal.

"Sun hounds!" I sang. "The Sun of Darkness is about to set. The Sun of Fire comes next in turn. The men of this creation are to be destroyed by a rain of fire, changed into hopping chickens and dogs."

"Are you mad, Considine?" came Amberson's voice, nearer now. "Look, I'm sorry I said what I did. I apologize. But, man—are you mad!"

Now that I'd turned off to the east I was driving slower, yet the buggy rocked and jolted over the broken-backed minor road, tossing us about like fish in a scaling drum.

"It bruises me!" cried Marina, shipwrecked, clinging to her seat.

Your white nudity, Marina—and the Earth's dark nudity to be explored, revealed!

"I give you the sun, you hounds and runners and presidents of this land!" I hurled the words into the babbling radiophone. And even Met Central was starting to show excitement, for they were listening too, and beginning to feed out data rapidly that vectored in on me and my position.

As I stared through the windshield, the greyness ahead slowly lightened to a misty white that spiralled higher and higher into the upper air. We could see fifty yards, a hundred yards ahead. A great light bubble was forming in the dark. In wonder and gratitude, I slackened speed.

We stopped.

"Thank God for that," muttered Marina.

"Considine here, you sun-hounds—you'd better come up fast, for I'm in the light-bubble now, it's rising, spiralling above, five minutes off the sun at most I'd say. It's big, this one."

"Is that the truth, Considine?" Amberson demanded.

"The truth? Who's nearest?" I called to the sun runners in general. And looked around. My buggy stood on a smashed stretch of road bandaging the blackened ground, at the base of a great funnel of strengthening light . . .

"Maybe I am." (Very loud, and breathlessly—as though running ahead of his buggy to catch me up.) "Harry Zammitt of Helios Hunters. I'm . . . coming into the fringes of it now. I see your buggy, Considine. The white whirlpool. Up and up! It's all true. Considine—I don't know how to say it. What you've done. Busting out, hunting down the sun in a matter of hours!"

As that first buggy bumped into the intensifying bubble of light, I piloted my own machine off the road onto the black ground.

We sat, watching the first rays of the sun burn through in golden shafts as the last mist melted.

And suddenly the day was on fire around us.

I squinted up through dark glasses and my windshield at a sun that seemed greater and brighter, a different color even, from any I'd ever seen before, steely whiter—as if there was less separating me from the sun, that day.

"Out," I ordered Marina, leaning over her bare legs to flip the door-lock open.

She stepped out obediently into the sunshine, while I gathered the obsidian knife up by the thong from under my seat, dropped it in my pocket.

"But it hurts," she cried in surprise—the hopping chicken with burnt feet, exactly! "It's too hot."

"Naturally the sun is hot."

Yes it was hot, so very hot. The hard hot rays burning at my skin the moment I stepped outside, hot as a grill, a furnace.

Harry Zammitt moved closer in his buggy, and other buggies were rolling into the sunspot now.

"Marina—you must stand against the buggy— no, better bend your body back, sprawl backwards over the hood, lie on it—but keep your eyes closed or you'll be blinded."

"You can't make love to me across a car," she whined feebly, moving in a daze, wincing as her body touched the heating metal. "It hurts."

"It's a buggy," said I. "Lie back, damn you, lover. Across the hood of my buggy."

"You animal, you primitive animal," she mumbled doing just as I said, spreading herself across the hood with her eyes screwed shut. For her this was the climax that confirmed all her fears and lusts for such scum as myself. Oh Marina!

For me the climax was different.

(Had I ever tried to warn you—had I? Who was I now, Considine the human being, or Considine the Priest of the Sun? Liar Considine, how you enjoyed being possessed—how you enjoyed the sanctification of your torture, in order to achieve the torture of sanctity—Marina!)

I, Considine, Priest of the Sun, snatched the obsidian knife from my pocket and brought it slashing down into your chest.

A pretty mess I made of you. The Aztecs must have had dozens of prisoners to practice on. At one blow! Monkeys maybe. Maybe they executed monkeys in the dark rooms under the temple pyramids. By the time I had hacked through the chaos of smashed ribs, torn breast muscle, flesh, that had been your body and my guide—by the time I had trapped the palpitating blood-sodden rag of your heart in my fist and wrenched it free—by that time I was vomiting onto the black soil.

(Soil that showed no signs of the flash harvest of grass and tiny blooms we all looked for, though it had been sprinkled with blood—as was I.)

My mouth putrid with bile, I turned, held your heart, Marina, high, dripping, to the blazing hurtful sun that blistered my skin raw as a flayed criminal's.

"What are you doing, Considine!" screamed the Magnificent Amberson, plunging toward me across the black earth—for he had finally got here, in the wake of some of his followers—sheltering himself under a sheet of metal.

"Sacrificing," said I. "As the sun god requires."

"Sun god?" he snarled.

"Tezcatlipoca has been reborn in the sky—surely you see?"

"Bloodthirsty maniac—I don't care about that—I can't see anything up there! Where has the ozone cover gone?"

I turned to Amberson then blankly, still clutching the wet heart.

"What?"

"The ozone layer in the upper air, don't you realize it's gone? Met Central is shouting murder about it. The hard radiation is getting through. You're burning to death if you stay out here. That's why there's no harvest, you fool. Scattering blood around isn't going to help!"

I dropped the heart on the ground, where it lay bubbling gently, tiny bubbles of blood, into the unresponsive warming soil.

Amberson snatched at me, maybe to drag me under the metal sheet with him, but I shook him off and jumped into my buggy, locked the doors, opaqued the windows.

And sat trembling there with the obsidian blade freshly blooded in my lap.

"Considine!" cried voices over the radiophone.

"Considine?" Amberson's voice—he was back in his sun buggy.

"Yes, I'm here."

"Now hear me, sun runners all, Considine led you here, and I admit I don't know how. But now maybe he'd like to explain why we can't go outside without being burnt, and where the harvest is?"

I said nothing.

"No? I'll tell you. Anyway, it's coming over Met

Central. The ozone layer in the upper air has finally broken down—the pollution has gotten to it and changed it—and as the ozone layer just happens to be what filters out the hard radiation from the sun, we had better get the hell out of here. Reflecting—as we do—on the demise of the honorable sport of the sun hunt. From now on anyone who spots the sun is going to wish himself a hundred miles away. So get going sun runners. And bugger you Considine. Let's all know this as Considine's Sunspot—the last sunspot anyone ever hunted for. A nice curse to remember a bloodthirsty fool by!"

Tezcatlipoca, why had you cheated me? Did her blood not flow like milk to your satisfaction? Was it because I botched the sacrifice so clumsily? Where the Aztec priest used one swift blow of the knife to unsheath the heart, I used twenty. . . .

One thing Amberson was wrong about. The biggest thing of all. The thing that has given me my present role, more hated than Amberson could ever have dreamed as he uttered his curse upon me.

For Considine's Sunspot was not going to close up, ever. It carried on expanding, taking in more acres hour by hour.

Far more than the ozonosphere had altered in those chemical mutations of the past few hours. The pall of dirt that had blanketed the Earth so many years was swift to change, whatever new catalyst it was that had found a home in the smog; now, starting at one point and spreading outward, the catalyst preceding (swimming like a living

thing—Snowflake's "childish" nightmare!) on a
wave front from the point of light, the changed
smog yielded to the hard radiations of the naked
sun.

I was right—which is the horror of it—I was
right. Tezcatlipoca is alive again, but no friend to
man. Nor was he ever friend to man, but cheated
and betrayed him systematically with his magic
and his song, and his stink. Tezcatlipoca, vicious
bear, hideous giant coming head in hand, bound-
ing jaguar, using me as focus for his flames, as
plainly as he used Marina (my lost love!) for his
map.

Considine's Sunspot spreads rapidly from one
day to the next, gathering strength, sterilizing
further areas of the country, burning the earth
clean. Algae beds consumed faster than they
can be covered over. Fuller domes shrivelling,
flimsy-fabricked. Buildings in flames, so brittle.
The asphalt motorways blazing fifty-mile-long
tinder strips.

So let me be Priest of the Burning World then,
since it is what I foretold and since, strangely (is it
so strangely in these fear-crazed times?), the cult
of Tezcatlipoca has revived, at least its ceremonies have, blood sacrifices carried out in the
polluted zones beyond the encroaching flame
front, in vain hopes of stemming it—oh, they only
add fuel to the sun's fire!—with their cockerels
and bullocks stolen from the zoo sheds . . . and
people too, captive and volunteer—beating hearts
torn out by far more expert hands than mine,
tossed blindly at where the sun burns its way
toward them. And, what no one will volunteer for,

the flame kindled in the darkness on someone's writhing scream-torn body, to impress the god of fire—Xiuhtecuhtli—oh yes, modern scholarship is on our side! And after further scholarly researches (did not witchcraft almost win a World War?) babies are cooked alive, eaten in honor of Tlaloc, god of rains and springs, who waters the earth. Outlaws and inlaws, bandits and wasps— we are all in this together, now.

My fate, Wandering Jew of the burning roads, is to lurk outward and ever outward, casting around the perimeter of Sunspot Considine, buggy rationed and fueled free of charge, with hatred, meeting up with my worshippers, torturers, meteorologists (has not meteorology absorbed all the other sciences?), time and again overcome by a craze of words bubbling from Tezcatlipoca's lips—taunts, demands, tricks and curses fluttering through my mouth from elsewhere, like captive birds set free, like the souls of his victims escaping into the sky.

And I ask:

Why me?

And:

Why you, Marina?

How I love you, in retrospect, having held your beating heart within my palm!

And the sunspot that bears my name, great tract of flameland seared into the world, pre-Cambrian zone of sun-scarred earth sterile except for the bacteria lying in waiting for some million-year-to-come event—do you realize that logically the whole world will bear my name one day, if the sunspot expands to embrace it, though no one

will be here to use the name—of Considine's
Planet (as it may be known to the ghosts upon
it)—why am I not allowed to drive in there and
die? But the mad sun god will not allow it, while
yet he holds me dangling on a string, jerking my
vocal chords as it amuses him. Since I plucked her
heart out I am his creature utterly. As she was
mine, and earlier still as I was hers. So it rolls
around.

Once I was a free man, sun hunter, outlaw. Now
a potential planet—and a slave. The empty gift
of omnipotence! Considine's world—naked pre-
Cambrian of some future society of insects, perhaps!

Marina.

Whose heart I felt flutter in my hand.

Thy blood like milk for me has flowed, hot as
iron pouring from a furnace!

Marina and Considine.

Eve and Adam of the world's end, our non-love
brought life to its close, victim and executioner of
the vanishing smogscape—which we all long for
nowadays, passionately, and would sacrifice anything, or anyone to bring it back to us.

This tale is for the sun god, Tezcatlipoca, with
my curses, and for you, Marina. . . .

SITTING ON A STARWOOD STOOL

Starwood. Imagine. It comes in very small slices. Approximately this, by this, by this. (Quick gestures with the hands.) They trade it out at Point Q which is to say at the intersection of reality with a mathematical equation—an idea more than a place, though we can both reach it. They ask whatever they want for it: ten kilos of a rare transuranium metal, the last surviving Botticelli, a few dozen beautiful boys and girls. Then they abolish the equation and vanish into oblivion (which is to say: into reality, somewhere else in the Galaxy or Magellanic Clouds), to reappear with another few slices of the wood after 1.23 terrestial years— maybe this says something about their home planet, or maybe nothing—probably it's a random number. No way of tracking them. No way of tracing the starwood world. They tell us it isn't anywhere near their home system, anyway . . .

Starwood. Just a single slice—sufficient for a stool. Or throne. Whether you're monk or monarch or whatever. But a very rich monk, need I say! Such as the head of the Japanese Yakuza Order . . .

A single slice—and if I'd stolen for ten years or worked honestly for 500, I'd still only have been able to travel to Point Q as a tourist to gawp at the building . . .

Starwood—they've told us this to prove its rarity—comes from a quirk of a planetoid called Toscanini, with an orbit the same as a comet's ellipse. Toscanini rushes in from the chill of deep space, soaks up the sunshine at perihelion for a few brief days then zips away again for long years in the icebox of far-out.

It ought to be no more than a ball of rock, too cold for any life-form to take root on for most of its orbit, then baked sterile in the oven. But life, once seeded, is ingenious. Toscanini has an ecology of trees that quarry metals from the rocks. Not just any metals—super-conducting metals that carry electrical activity on forever at the few degrees above absolute zero that the planet's surface reduces to through most of its flight.

Those trees on Toscanini live through the years of the freeze, powered by organic batteries that never run down. At perihelion, when the trees are being baked in the star's heat, they soak up the energy to power their batteries; then while the planet is scooting away through deep space again, the trees put out their shoots and saplings and new growth rings, radiating the surplus energy they've stored into the immediate vicinity to nourish them. It's such a life-enhancing energy that the whole Toscanini wood would be suffocated under tons of parasites if the planet didn't rush close enough to its sun to scour it clean of competition . . .

Why "Toscanini" for a name? I've heard it said that their starship captain who first found the world and its strange organic metal trees had a taste for Earth music, and a sense of humor, and recalled a "super conductor" from centuries ago . . .

But the remarkable thing about starwood is this. If you sit on it, it radiates its energies into you. And it rejuvenates any human being. A properly cut and tailored piece of starwood recharges the mitochondria (the powerhouses) in the cells. It tones up the brain waves. It balances the Yin and Yang. A chess-player squatting on starwood is unbeatable. A philosopher can work out the universal truths in his head. A businessman can build empires. It's the ultimate conditioner. Hair grows back—even brain cells regenerate. The impotent recover their virility. The immune system can eat up any cancer, however metastasized. But they can only harvest mature trees—for a large enough cross-section of the superconductor circuits—and the trees grow back so slowly there on Toscanini, so they say.

(Pardon me if I sound like a promotional tape. Truly, they have no need to promote starwood vulgarly. And the likes of I, no means of buying it . . .)

Even so, I'd hardly have dared try to steal the Grand Monk of the Yakuza's stool from under him, hadn't I found I had a cancer, inoperable, irreversible, metastasizing plaguefully through me. Then all thoughts of virility and playing chess and planning the perfect crimes washed out of me, leaving me with the one glaring imperative: to save my life by the most risky theft of all.

The Yakuza are Buddhist monks, somewhere on the martial side of Zen—enlightenment through archery, swordsmanship, and other death-arts. They are also, each and every one, part of the great gangster fraternity underpinning whole commercial empires: the Benevolence Company. Yet a Jakuza is as earnestly philosophical as he is deft at protecting himself as he is potentially thuggish, in the old strict meaning of the word. A paradox. But Zen is a bird's nest of paradoxes, and the Yakuza are no exception. So the Grand Monk, sitting on his heap of gold and starwood—which he has fought his way to, through blinding enlightenments of backstreet duels and assassinations, is also author of one of the great works of religious thought of this age: *The Way of the Milky Way*—a fine, wise book.

But at least I could get to see the Grand Monk, to consult him on a point of philosophy, if I laid enough bribes "along the way" and a large enough cash donation to the Benevolence Company at his feet. All quite in order. All quite normal. The same as a personal audience with the Roman Pope, amongst his Swiss guards.

He would be guarded, of course. The Yukuza being martial craftsmen, in this age that means solid state circuitry as well as the old perfect equipoise of mind and muscle . . . I hadn't realized all the implications, though. It was worse, far worse than I'd expected and I had to go through with it, when I got to the point. My weapons had an expire deadline on them. I'd arranged it that way, so that I shouldn't just mumble something about philosophy and then back out . . .

A crazy, mad venture, in retrospect; but then, at
the back of my mind, I thought I'd be safe forever if
only I toppled him from his starwood stool and
squatted there myself, however briefly. An almost
mystical, magic obsession!

I had, of course, also planned escape routes.

I had, of course, watched all available tapes of
the Grand Monk in audience with "parishion-
ers". Counted and recounted the small team of
swordsmen attending him. Always three, and
only three.

I had, of course, expected a battery of sniff-
snoops and scan-screens, on the way to him . . .
They wouldn't fight guns with swords—even if I
had seen one tape of a Yakuza deflecting high-
speed pellets with his sword's edge, after an
hour's meditation on the stool . . . My weapons
were undetectable. I'd stolen the specifications
for them two years before from an eccentric inven-
tor far away, whom I'd afterwards had to strangle.
I was fairly sure they'd work. I'd saved them for
this day.

My nerve and flesh grenades were woven of
poly-ice—the alternative coherent form of water
that can be tied into knots like wire as soon as it
spins out of a freezer's capillary tubes. These were
hidden in a row down my lapel, like a jewelled
decoration. The index and middle fingers of both
my hands had thin woven ice capsules implanted
in them with ice lenses primed to emit one single
beam of laser fire if I cocked my finger and
pointed it.

Within three hours after manufacture I had to
use these weapons before they grew incoherent,
and used themselves on me. As I walked into the

Grand Monk's room, I had just thirty minutes left
. . . As I say, I had no choice but to proceed . . .

The Grand Monk had a fat, poachy white face,
with eyes sunk deep in hoods of milky flesh. He
must have been 150 years old with an infantile
yoghurty complexion. His thick red and blue
brocade robes tied with a white cord thick as a
bell-rope, and his white linen cap, I recognized
well enough from the tapes. His suite, too, fur-
nished with stern luxury. The *tatami* matting
with its black borders. The few scrolls. The
picture-window set to display a misty flight of
geese through an emptiness intruded upon by a
few gravity-defying cliffs. Data bank within arm's
reach of the stool he sat on, entirely enveloping
this in his robes . . .

The stool, the stool is under *that* mass . . . !

I was intoxicated. I could already feel it healing
me, invigorating me—emanating through his
body and clothes . . . He had his bare flesh
pressed to the starwood, under that red and blue
brocade, I had no doubt . . . white buttocks in
interface with the metal tree of Toscanini in a
reversal of entropy, as though a living star *defe-
cated* energy into him . . . He disgusted me already. I could smell his flesh sizzling . . .

Something missing.

The three swordsmen!

Something else present.

A great dog . . . !

I stared at the creature. It sprawled, twice the
size of a wolfhound, behind his stool, chin on its
paws. Its nostrils flared, its ears pricked back, its
tongue lolled out to taste me, a single eye opened

to regard me. And its paws were human hands, with steel claws.

The eye shut, and the other eye opened.

It began to blink in sequence, rapidly.

One eye shut, one eye open.

Its sides were armored like a rhino's. Its body rippled with hauser muscles of spun steel, as it stretched itself. I shrank into a solid knot of ice, inside.

"The cyb-hound," intoned the Grand Monk. "A fresh product of the Benevolence Company. But you came to ask about philosophy, not to buy protection."

I held my donation slackly, wrapped in the correct scarlet ribbon, tied such and such a way. (Quick gestures with the hands.)

The proper procedure was, I should lay it in front of him on the empty wooden tray there— within half a meter of those grafted hands with metal claws!

I hesitated briefly.

I understood the rapid on-off blinking of the dog's eyelids well enough now . . . This surgical intersection of body and machine lolling there was impregnable to any ordinary sword, gun or grenade. My finger lasers would have to hit the beast direct through the eyes to short out its cyb-brain! And the eyelids would be high-reflective steel. Which was why its eyes shone like mirrors as it shut them and a nictitating barrier shot across.

Almost impossible.

I had twenty-six minutes before my woven ice uncohered and ravaged me.

So I laid my donation, carefully, at the Grand Monk's feet, squinting under his robes sleazily at the feet of the stool, like some young virgin boy standing under a transparent stairway to squint up skirts; and engaged the Grand Monk in talk . . . about what I remembered from *The Way of the Milky Way*. (It was a completely crazy venture, I knew now, but what choice had I?)

His hooded eyes regarded me pertly.

The cyb-hound's gaze flickered at me. And it dragged itself slowly upright, savoring my fear with its tongue on the very air . . . I'd painted my sweat glands over with a monomolecular filter, to fool the normal anxiety sniffers . . . but I couldn't block its animal sense for the essential taste of the situation, enhanced in the womb-vats, and souped up in the Yakuza craft-shop, so I imagined. (And all my imaginations only made matters worse. I wasn't a true assassin, only a skilful thief . . . and I believe even an assassin would have been bested by this beast . . . Not that any group or organization would have dreamt of assassinating the Grand Monk. I was mad, I realize now . . .)

"In *The Way of the Milky Way* you say—"

"Yes?"

And the cyb-hound launched itself at me . . .

Which is the true horror of it.

For the Grand Monk's robes parted as he shifted, cross-legged, on the stool, and I saw his raw flesh in contact with the wood of Toscanini; I drank in the wood vicariously, voyeuristically— and saw the location of the knot in it.

Like wood from most worlds, starwood has

knots where the branches have been lopped off the main trunk section . . .

As I say, the stool's superconductor rings leak star energy slowly upward into the bodily metabolism. Yet knots in the wood are secondary circuits. They have to be sealed off, or would upset the balance of the energy release. Thus ergs and ergs of power are locked up in a knot—ergs that can be released abruptly, all at once, in a tight jet along the line of the former branch, a hundred times as ravenous as a finger laser.

Of course, it ruins the wood. The stool's as spoilt as a cracked bell, afterwards . . .

The cyb-hound's front paws were off the ground now, and it hung in mid-air. (How time slowed down, as though the very glimpse of starwood immortalized that moment!)

I cocked the index and middle fingers of my right hand and flexed them at the knot, shattering the woven ice.

And shut my eyes.

And danced to the left of the room.

Already phantom steel-clawed hands were rending my ribs out, and steel-fanged claws drinking my neck dry . . . !

Except that . . . they didn't reach me. Didn't touch me.

Only a blinding light turned my shut eyelids to pools of blood . . . that abruptly darkened, in a howl.

I looked again.

For another long, frozen second the cyb-hound hung between me and the stool—black body eclipsing a blaze of light.

The knot had micro-novaed. A plume of star energy was spearing the dog's hide. Burning, melting its armor flesh. Shorting out its electronics.

I retained a retinal image of the dog shape silhouetted against the world, long after the body crashed to the mat . . .

"His left hand too!" I heard the blinded Grand Monk squealing, his brocade on fire. And there were others in the room.

And truly I felt no pain as, with a flicker, a swordsman cut off my fingers, and batted them towards a waste chute with the flat of his blade while they were still falling, barely detached from my hand.

I wouldn't have used them anyway, now.

The wood was ruined. I only wept.

And wept.

Later, I wept more, intoning these words to atone for the starwood spoilt—as ruined as a last T'ang porcelain vase thrown from the fortieth floor to the pavings. Intoning, and weeping. Weeping and atoning.

Worse, was when they forced me on to the stool itself, and I felt waves of unbalanced nausea radiating upward from it, for hour after hour . . .

For day after day, while I died, and died . . . and the stool kept me alive through all these deaths, fingerless, cancerous, malign metabolism fed by the energy of the far star that feeds the Toscanini trees, which I had so sickened and warped . . .

For week after week.

For month after month, until, my cancers in perfect harmony with the disharmony I brought about, I am pure, perfect, deathless cancer. A living tumor, chained to this cross-section of the steel tree in the Yakuza Temple. Atoning. For I realize that the Way of the Milky Way is truly the Way of Starwood—the living energy of stars passing into Man . . . And Starwood is the Way of Enlightenment in Agony, for me, sitting bound on this broken block.

Sometimes, the Grand Monk, wearing black lenses, comes down into the Temple to talk to me about my mental progress, and observe my vast, metastasized, pullulating body.

His retinas are growing back quickly now that the Benevolence Company have traded for a fresh slice of starwood out at Point Q.

He tells me they gave the last surviving Piero della Francesca in the world for it.

Starwood. Imagine. Comes in such small slices. Approximately this, by this, by this. (Quick gestures with two stumps sprouting ten tumors—soft red boiled carrots . . .)

I am even sitting on some.

AGORAPHOBIA, A.D. 2000

The Japanese astronaut Yamaguchi waited while the masked officials unsealed the 130-acre Shinjuku Gyoen Park, the sole remaining open space in the Tokyo megalopolis. They lifted the warning barriers aside, broke the seal on the padlock, inserted the ceremonial iron key. The corroded wicket swung open. The analogue of Mars lay before him.

Almost, but not quite.

For the main gate opened into the European-style court, designed by a Frenchman, Henri Martinet. This gravel court, flanked by the tall knobbled skeletons of dead trees, sloped uphill at an angle of ten degrees before leading out on to the open tableland of the park proper, effectively blocking this off from view.

"Remember, the first hundred meters are the easiest, Yamaguchi," the familiar voice of the Mission Director warned him over his helmet radio, stiff and formal with the seriousness of the occasion, the tipsy camaraderie of the farewell party forgotten, as it should be. "Don't be deceived. It looks just like a road. But it's a road to nowhere . . ."

A road? Yamaguchi looked around him. Yes, the stretch of scattered gravel certainly did resemble a torn-up road or under-road somewhere in the City. And the tall knobbly trees, they would be utility poles branching with insulators, surge diverters, cross arms . . . or perhaps the fifty-meter tall steel screws which scooped out the ground before piles could be driven for new buildings. The rows of dead trees stood ready to rip holes in the earth, to hammer in the pins for buildings, and more buildings—cancelling the absurdity of empty space with objects, with meaning.

The Space Agency officials stood back, keeping their eyes fixed on Yamaguchi to avoid looking at the expanse of the European Court sliding uphill at an angle of ten degrees towards—nowhere.

He stepped through the wicket and his boots crunched the gravel as he started uphill.

And a voice whispered in his mind, as he remembered the Code of Behavior.

"This is the day for you to commit hara-kiri. The weather is fine and the day is auspicious. May you be able to commit hara-kiri without any difficulty . . ."

At the top of the slope he paused and gazed ahead. The dead trees here formed a wide arc surrounding the final zone of gravel. Beyond this lay a desert of dry white crab-grass, smooth and uniform, opening out in all directions away from him, pushing the massed buildings of the City absurdly far away, creating an impossible bubble of space in the very midst of the City. The sheer pressure of this space! It could hold back all those millions of tons of steel and concrete without faltering! Yamaguchi walked out across the final zone of gravel, and thought he heard it vibrate like a tight-stretched drum. But it was only his own blood drumming, pounding. Telemetry would be recording his leaping pulse on a graph outside the park for the benefit of Space Science.

Then he stepped off gravel on to the desert of grass itself and the crunch-crunch sound of his boots vanished, leaving only the booming of his blood, and the distant booming of the City, coming from far away, yet meshing with his own blood and comforting him, for he was a man of the City. He walked on over the springy turf, sending no radio messages now and receiving none. The Code said: "*Whenever any conversation is attempted by the hara-kiri performer, 'Put your mind at rest' is the stereotyped response usually given; indulgence in conversation might only serve to disquieten the mind . . .*" Telemetry alone would monitor his progress and his physical and mental state.

The sun shone down weakly through the smog out of the blue of outer space, transforming the desert's surface of white grass into a vast gently-curving convex mirror. . . .

He wasn't conscious of having climbed any significant incline since leaving the shelter of the European Court, yet suddenly he seemed to be above the world, perched on this convex mirror which began to turn beneath him. Now the City seemed equidistant from him on all sides, though he had only penetrated a short distance into the park. He seemed not to have moved any nearer to his goal—that far horizon of buildings with red and white checked balloons floating over them—yet the European Court, when he glanced back, had shifted into the remote distance. His eyes were not playing tricks on him, he knew. It was just that judging such great distances as these was outside the present experience of Man. His hours in the simulator did not help him much, though they doubtless staved off nausea.

The background boom of the City was the grinding of the globe as it turned beneath him like a giant's clockwork toy. He felt dizzy. Then perspective did begin to play tricks on him. The scene leapt in at him, then bounced away. He was a giant perched on a tiny globe, terrified of falling off into endless space. He was a mouse scurrying across an immense plain while overhead an invisible hand groped for him from the sky. He felt a desperate need to take cover in the tunnels of the City. A moment later he was a giant again, dwarfing the City at the end of the plain, terrified that gravity might be *turned off*. In free fall he would float up into the endless sky. Every human being in the City was close enough to something to hold on to, but not him. There were only a few dead saplings a hundred meters away. Or was it a thousand meters?

The Code of Behavior said: *"Hara-kiri is not a mere suicidal process; it is a refinement of self-destruction and none can perform it without the utmost coolness of temper and composure . . ."*

Why then was Yamaguchi running, stumbling along in his thick rubber boots and bulky suit, panting like a dog on a hot day while they witnessed his humiliation through their remotely controlled telescopes slung from those distant balloons?

He ran to the nearest tree. Like a dog he felt compelled to urinate against it. Of course, the urine flowed into a special bag strapped to his thigh. There was no risk of it running down his leg. Still, he imagined that it was running down his leg, and felt ashamed.

"A hara-kiri performer should tuck his sleeves beneath his knees to prevent himself from falling backwards . . ."

Without the weight of his spacesuit he would float up into the sky; without his spacesuit's all-enveloping life-support system he would fly apart explosively.

The small white sun beat down through the haze on to this dead bent tree, casting a shadow that could be used to tell the time if he stayed here long enough. The silence was a huge blob of clear jelly that conducted only a faint throb from the distant City, the fading rhythm of his own existence. . . .

At last, torn between shame and fear, Yamaguchi trudged off in a direction chosen at random, perhaps retracing his steps, but most likely not. He had lost touch with the horizon now. It mocked him with its faintness, equidistance, similarity.

Soon the sun was shrinking and the smog haze closing in. The neon signs that had sprung to life over the City only made the desert seem darker and more hideous. Yamaguchi almost walked past the flat disc set in the grass without noticing it.

It was a tree stump sawn off flush with the ground, with a wire handle fixed to it.

But, of course! There had to be something underneath the Park! Subterranean passages, underground factories, transit tubes. If the Park was just something laid on top of part of the City's body, like a mat, then there was nothing to be afraid of. The City was *here* as well as *there*. He could raise this lid. Discover a ladder leading down to safety. How many lids there must be, concealed about the park. He would never have seen one had he marched in a straight line from gate to gate. But he had wandered off course. It was just an illusion that he was *outside* the City trapped in some obscene bubble of unnatural force!

The bulky spacesuit prevented him from bending over or kneeling down. However, he had a telescopic probe in his instrument pocket for taking soil samples, which he now took out, extended, and hooked through the wire handle.

The tree-stump wasn't heavy, it was only a few centimeters thick.

Underneath was a small pit with cement walls, leading nowhere. At the bottom of the pit sat a steel globe with knives and shears and clippers sticking out of it like arms. As the fading light struck its sensors, it appeared to move slightly. Shears to snip tentatively. A knife to rotate. He had stumbled on one of the robot-gardeners in its nest.

The shock of encountering life—or what appeared to be life—in this wilderness, made him drop the telescopic probe, and run, anywhere . . .

And now the desert spread around him desolate and absurd, becoming a black void as the sun disappeared.

Before exhaustion overwhelmed him he located another tree, took the umbilical tether from his instrument pocket, and, fumbling with his clumsy gloves, fastened one end of the cord to his waist and the other to the tree trunk. Carefully, so as not to damage his suit, he lowered himself to the ground, paying the cord out slowly.

Later, as Yamaguchi slept fitfully, the Moon rose, and the robot-gardener, fully alert now, climbed out of its cement pit and rolled towards the astronaut, tracking him by his body-heat.

When it reached him, it extruded its sharpest knife, plunged the blade through his suit and into his abdomen. Without a moment's delay it dragged the blade across his belly from left to right, then, turning the knife in the wound, made a brief upward cut.

As Yamaguchi thrashed about in hideous pain, fastened within the cumbersome spacesuit, the robot raked him over on to his belly and extruded a long curved sword with a shining blade. Swiftly the sword slashed through his neck, a little below the plexiglass helmet.

The Code said: *"It is considered expert not to cut the head completely off in one stroke, but to leave a portion of uncut skin at the throat . . ."*

Yamaguchi had failed; nonetheless he met an honorable death.

Back at the Space Agency Center outside the Park, beyond the court designed by Henri Martinet, now locked and sealed again, the telemetry officials noted the termination of life functions, as well as the sudden surge of readings just before the end.

PROGRAMMED LOVE STORY

Once upon a time in the year Two Thousand there
will be a hostess in the Queen Bee cabaret
in Tokyo, called Kei. Her marriage to a young
businessman has turned out sadly. He has quar-
relled with her. And why? Because he is convinced she has the wrong personality. She is
pretty, yes. She is graceful and tactful, yes. They
make love with all the proficiency and enthu-
siasm that Dr. Sha Kokken had prescribed. But
as his business prospects grow he has grown
superstitious—and the firm's astrology computer
has lately whispered in his ear that she is wrong
for him. That they should have taken more heed of
their horoscopes (which modern science, increasingly conscious of the existence of patterns in
the universe, has validated by the year Two
Thousand) and less of romantic love. That her
palm print is incompatible with his—a fact that he
never noticed while they were courting and holding hands. That her grace and softness will hold
him back, for what the firm needs during the
coming millenium is tough aggressive managers
for overseas, with tough aggressive wives to goad
them on. So he has grown bitter towards her,
reproaching her for her tender and yielding
(though amorous) nature, exhorting her day by

day to reform her personality, to change herself—
though into what she has to change herself he has
never quite made up his mind. And this has gone
on until one sad day, simply because she loves
him and would not stand in his way, she has left
him.

Once upon a time in the year Two Thousand
there will be a woman called Kei who works as a
cabaret hostess to support herself, though even in
the year Two Thousand the pay at the Queen Bee
is not so good considering the nature of the services demanded . . .

Only a stone's throw away from Nihonbashi
Bridge which travellers used to set off from in the
old days in papanquins borne by high-stepping
servants on their way to Kyoto, which modern
man sets off from in neon-striped taxis with automatic doors on the fifty-seven stages of extrava-
gance known as the Ginza; only a stone's throw
away from where the metal dragons of the bridge
rear their heads (though only just) between the
lanes of the overhead expressway—is the Queen
Bee's extensive, if shabby, facade. By the year
Two Thousand the Queen Bee has done her dam-
nedest to keep up with the times.

Kei's pliant yielding nature—if it did not seem
to qualify her very well for life with her husband
the Almost Twenty-First Century Businessman
—did uniquely qualify her for work at the
Queen Bee.

Today when a customer walks into that cabaret,
he is handed a computer sheet showing twenty
situations—modest traditional bride, brisk nurse
tending the wounded war hero, sailor-suited
schoolgirl presenting an apple to the teacher, fat

nude trussed up tightly so that her flesh bulges over the ropes like the Michelin tire man . . . he marks the four scenes he likes best, in order of preference; the computer locates her closest to his heart among the hundred hostesses.

By the year Two Thousand the Queen Bee has installed a far more sophisticated computer of the SWARM variety—a Suggestibility Wizard & Rapport Machine. As soon as the customer (honored guest, as they say) has chosen the face he fancies from the catalogue of a hundred pretty faces, and the personality type he yearns for from the pack of a hundred situation cards—take note that a hundred pretty faces multiplied by a hundred personalities will give him the choice of ten thousand women—the owner of the pretty face is summoned to the changing room. Suppose that the pretty face is Kei's, she will need all her pliant yielding nature then, for only a genuine yielding nature can accept the Suggestibility Wizard & Rapport Machine's imprinting of a fresh personality upon it without giving signs of a schizophrenia distressing to an honored guest.

Once upon a time in the year Two Thousand there will be a hostess called Kei upon whose brain a Suggestibility Wizard & Rapport Machine imposes a fresh personality nightly—which is to say up until two a.m. in the morning when the Queen Bee shuts up shop and a hundred hostesses, passing through the front door onto the Ginza, pass through an eraser field too and find themselves out there among the neon lights, dehypnotized, with memories of being other people, so many miniskirted high-heeled swamis dreaming of reincarnation . . .

Once upon a time in the year Two Thousand a pliant gentle personality will be a prior essential for any girl who wants to be a Queen Bee hostess and adopt personalities which are not hers, personalities that need not themselves be particularly pliant or gentle . . . (For does not Situation Card 64 depict a leather-clad lady whipping her escort with a riding crop?)

Once upon a time in the year Two Thousand there will be a rising young businessman called Kenzo whose status with the firm ensures his section chief taking him along precisely once a month to some cabaret or other to entertain clients into the wee hours of the morning, all expenses paid . . .

Thus one evening in the year Two Thousand this Kenzo will walk into the Queen Bee along with his section chief and a client from Kyoto and be handed a catalogue of a hundred pretty faces, among which he is mildly surprised to find his wife Kei. Now whether it was Kenzo's reluctance to watch his wife entertaining strangers, or whether he had decided to play a practical joke upon her (his bitterness not having entirely abated yet), he chose this particular face from among the hundred to be his hostess; and from the pack of cards selected number 78—Strength in High Places, the Imperial Concubine.

The transistor hidden in her brassiere gave a beep summoning Kei to the changing room, where she submitted herself obediently to the Suggestibility Wizard & Rapport Machine, emerging a few moments later with arrogance and precision, cruel, bent on power, mind hatching devious plots, mostly centered on the swift rise to a

position of eminence of her new protégé, whom
she would shortly meet, cajole, mold and entice.
For the whiskies she pressed on her victim at 100
New Yen a shot were transactions of great significance; the colored water she drank herself (at
100 New Yen a shot) a clever way of evading the
poisoner's art.

One upon a time in the year Two Thousand
a rising businessman will summon his lost wife
before him in the image of the Imperial Concubine—and she will cajole him, mold him, entice him, under the envious eyes of his Section
Chief, till he sighs: "What such a woman could do
for me!" and falls helplessly in love with her . . .

Long after midnight, when the Section Chief
had paid Queen Bee for their night's entertain-
ment and Kenzo is travelling home in a neon taxi
with stereo chansons playing softly, he still loves
her helplessly and thinks about her; for poetic
justice cuts both ways.

The next night on his own he made his way
back to the Queen Bee, pointed at that pretty face
in the catalogue, and asked for personality
number 78.

Sitting opposite the Imperial Concubine,
watching with dismay how fast she drained the
glasses of colored water, Kenzo cried out at last:

"Do you know who I am, Kei?"

And she smiled the Austere Perfection Smile
appropriate to the castration ceremonies of court
eunuchs; and nodded.

"Do you know I am your husband?"

"Husband?" She laughed lightly, a laugh appropriate to an enemy's execution reported earnestly by a doting prince.

"With you by my side—*this* you—I could climb
so high . . ."

The prospect of power . . . she leaned forward.

"Shall I inform you how to twist that Section
Chief of yours round your little finger? Did you
take note which girl he chose? What she represented?"

Shamed, he shook his head.

"You should have noticed—for that was the key
to his soul."

"I was too busy noticing you, my darling wife."

"Nonsense! I am an imperial concubine—you
know we can never be wed. We can only meet in
safety as conspirators."

Once upon a time in the year Two Thousand
there will be a rising young businessman who
conceives an obsession for the Imperial Concubine of the Queen Bee, to whom he was once
married, and woos her a second time, spending all
his salary, then all his savings, on glasses of
whisky-colored water, and little dishes of rice
crackers . . . and still her heart—in that incar-
nation—is chiselled out of rice.

And early every morning at 2 a.m. after his
fruitless visits she walks out, dehypnotized, onto
the Ginza, weeping at the Imperial Concubine's
inability to thaw, and yield.

In the year Two Thousand, on the Ginza, once
upon a time there will be a benighted businessman who has gone so deep into debt that
he embezzles thousands of New Yen from his firm
to pay the Queen Bee, till his Section Chief dis-
covers and fires him; who goes with his last pock-
etful of change to spend it on colored water and
rice crackers for an Imperial Concubine he is sure

is at last on the very point of yielding.

Once upon a time on the Ginza there will be a tender yielding hostess, Kei by name, who submits to a Suggestibility Wizard & Rapport Machine nightly, till one night she submits to it no more . . . who elopes from the Queen Bee with her protégé, passing through an erasure field as she leaves the door, to become . . .

"Oh Kenzo!"

"Oh Kei!"

. . . the tough hard wife of a ruined ex-businessman, with whom she walks along the Ginza through the neon forest—for they can't afford a taxi fare—till at last they come to Shimbashi Station where the shoeshine people have left their equipment out overnight—who would steal shoeshine equipment?

In the year Two Thousand there will be a tough handsome couple shining people's shoes in the early morning as the trains rattle overhead and the neon taxis swing past. You can still see this couple, older now and beginning to suffer from chest trouble from the exhaust fumes, shining and repairing shoes on the street by Shimbashi Station through the night. If you look for them carefully. Once upon a time in the future.

This story is brought to you by a Suggestibility Wizard & Rapport Machine programmed to print out stories about itself suitable for junior high schools during the slack periods of the day, by courtesy of the management, Queen Bee Cabaret, Tokyo, tax-deductible for educational purposes.

We do not sell merchandise; we sell human nature.

THE GIRL WHO WAS ART

Who else can recreate with her body the immortal works of Tadanori Yokoo, morning star of Japan's economic sunrise in the mid-Twentieth century, quite as myself? Gazing at his superbly ironic body on pages 18 and 19 of the priceless first edition of *Posthumous Works* (presented to me by my Master as a necessary part of my equipment) I can sense his petulant eyes and surly lips meeting mine across the years. T lies alone on a maroon paisley bed, posters pasted on the walls, body propped on a slim elbow . . . and if I were able to travel back in time and knock on his door I'd open my mouth wide as a lockjaw moon and hold that pose till he was amazed, compelled to pout in his bored way, "Well I guess I can use your face"— he'd never guess that neither lockjaw nor lock-anything can cramp my style after the hours of muscle-training I've undergone.

Admittedly false pride can ruin a good performer who has to be quite selfless when she comes to submerge herself in her role. Yet how can I help feeling just a little proud of being the best interpreter of T in all Japan? For I know I am. No one has devoted more to her art. Is this pride? I don't think so. My only joy is to feel what flowers must have felt in the gone days of Ikebana, had they been gifted with consciousness: the fulfillment of being part of a design. For I am an intelligent flower that has the privilege of arranging itself—according to T's immortal graphic designs, prescient patterns of our new Japan to which the whole world turns.

My Master is a man of taste—one of the first businessmen to turn away from the old artists of a dead world, those Manets and Rubenses and Utamaros, leaving the girls who specialized in creating them to drag their wasted talents round country fairs and department store roofs. But the etiquette of praise is very strict. We feel that open praise is a little vulgar. That is for foreigners to lavish. My Master cannot exactly praise my nightly performances—in fact he must sit with his back to them, in the place of honor. Only when he has a guest to dinner can he sit facing me across the table and take notice of me. I may also hear a word of praise from the guest. Yet it isn't praise or fame that I think about as I hold my pose there perfectly still. Am I worthy of T and his design? That's all I wonder.

My Master usually phones immediately after lunch so that I can be in place when he gets home in the evening. Apart from the *Posthumous Works* open in front of me as I wait for his call, my room is perfectly bare. The costume cupboards closed, everything neat. My whole life being in here, I want nothing to distract me from T's ideas. Here I eat and here I sleep and on my holiday here I often remain, meditating. Rarely do I open the paper screen windows. What need is there to? It's all in T's own work, foreseen so many years ago—the blazing highrise buildings, the trains with giant plastic flowers sprouting from them, the crashing helicopters, naked girls globed in fishbowl helmets, lunar city under the smoking volcano, rays of the sun diffracted into broad red beams by the smog and skyscrapers, our flag spread open in the sky at last for visitors from abroad to wonder at. . . .

Last night I posed in the cool crazy White Smile from that vintage year 1966: stooping in front of the white china toilet with the split seat, bowing with a big toothy grin, my slip hanging off one shoulder showing both breasts, bending over to pull my red knickers down below my knees . . .

The night before I was a New York Girl in a brown wig with curls, my left arm sticking straight up in the air waving above a smudge of brown armpit, right hand grasping a telephone speaker to a mouth red with lipstick, bright vermilion tongue sticking out cheekily over my lower lip—and my huge eyes blank white contact-lens cut-outs in my face. The telephone dial-box hanging down by my waist, ballooning red skirt pinned neatly to it, showing off my sky-blue knickers, black suspenders, a blue stocking and a red stocking, against a backdrop of mid-air Manhattan with a blond beachguard cutout appraising me . . .

Earlier in the week, I was the girl jockey bent double over my black plastic steed with my hair streaming in the wind and a fresh mackerel clasped between my teeth.

I've stood nude before Mt. Fuji with my hair done up in a towel, teeth in a foam of tingling toothpaste.

I've been the bare-breasted vampire at the seaside. I've been the Japanese Mona Lisa squeezing a jet of milk—thin white plastic strand—from one nipple while my other hand toys with my clitoris inside my white panties, mouth wide open, eyes rolled upwards, flowing golden mane, masturbating maniac of the rocks . . .

The telephone buzzes.

My Master appears on the screen, I bow to him, he nods a quick acknowledgment.

"I have a guest tonight . . . Kindly do The Gratitude of Aeschylus." And breaks the connection, vanishing in the whirlpool of his own light, busy man.

My heart leaps with joy, for The Gratitude of Aeschylus is one of the most complex, most demanding, most aesthetically satisfying of all T's works. I shall need all the time there is.

Adding cream dye to the already hot water in my bath behind the sliding door, I submerge myself totally, closing my eyes and breathing through a straw while I run down all the details of this demanding role . . .

Like a ballerina on tiptoes with legs wide apart I shall have to stand, pointed toes concealed in blue rubber mermaid fins that cling to my legs as far as the knees. Apart from a red Noh mask taped to my crotch, my only other article of dress is a diving helmet with an abnormally broad glass window. The air-hose from this coils round my body under my left breast, down behind my thigh, back between my legs, before doubling into the mouth of the Noh mask . . . the spectator sees the pipe as entering my vagina, is supposed to believe I'm breathing out of my own womb—the ultimate

self-sufficiency. In reality the hose passes between the tightness of my buttocks and is taped to
the small of my back. You can imagine how much
muscle control it takes to maintain this pose—
tiptoes, legs wide straddled, sucking in oxygen all
the way up that long hose, without giving any
sign of doing so!

A background rich in objects and flourishes.
Five red plastic butterflies, an apple tree with a
half dozen chewed apple cores and a blue serpent,
a vermilion devil with a flintlock rifle squeezing
his wife's nipple, a blazing nude stabbing her
Hindu lover while a headless wedding guest
stands by in a frock-coat, with a gravedigger in a
yellow T-shirt; and in the distance those twin
obsessions of the 1960s, the Moon and a nuclear
mushroom—oh so many things, such richness! I
have to put out flat plastic models of all these
things while the dye is drying on me. Flat, because two-dimensionality is an essential part of
The Gratitude of Aeschylus, unlike *White Smile*
which called for a three-dimensional toilet bowl
. . . and I too must seem flat and two-
dimensional, my widespread legs in the same vertical plane as my body, which isn't easy—believe
me—even for a specialist. . . .

In place, on tiptoe, in green fins, legs straddled,
eyes wide open, seeing everything bathed in
green by my contact lenses . . . not heeding the
dinner party, where is it? might make my eyes
flicker with curiosity create some nervous excitement betray itself in a twitch or flush.

Many ways of blanking attention during the

hours of the pose, for me precious hours, when identical with T's concepts of The Woman. Let mnemonic jingles loose in my head or advertising lyrics. Silently chant mantras and sutras. Mouth the syllable OM mentally. . . . Consider koans, what is the sound of one hand clapping. Attempt to reach a million by counting up in tens. Start a tape-loop of thoughts swinging round my head, doesn't matter what they are. Start telling myself a story, about anything, never get beyond the opening lines, over and over in new forms seeking perfection. Visualize a light year. Hypnotize myself by staring at a light or a shiny surface till the whole room fades out, only the bright light fills the universe, float up to meet it weightless bodiless. All these techniques taught in Image School.

This is a tape-loop of thoughts, doesn't matter what they are, in place, on tiptoe in green fins, legs straddled, eyes wide open, seeing everything . . . not heeding . . .

Round the table they're eating raw live lobster, shells stripped away from neatly-diced foamy pink backs, from which they pluck tiny cubes of flesh with their lacquer chopsticks, intact feelers questing the air vaguely, leg joints flexing in and out gently in a parody of motion.

The lady of the house kneels on the mats beside each man in turn, splashing Johnnie Walker Black Label into the tiny porcelain cups.

The guest, drinking, not eating as much as he ought to, art expert revered by everyone, has been like a father to his corpulent host; who is red-faced and always looks overheated as if somebody is busy cooking him, who secretly prefers a hand of poker.

"So you're still with this Yokoo brought-to-life thing?"

Quietly smirking.

Turning a shade redder with concern, the gas-ring under him hotting up, the host looks worried sick. Mistake to say "Why yes, shouldn't I be?"

"Maybe the market is turning against him," he theorizes, trying to catch the guest's suggestion on the wing. If I'm fast I can swap her with one of my less enlightened friends? Hot tips in art are so hard to understand, harder than the *I Ching's* hexagrams as used in business.

"Now I didn't say anything was wrong with Yokoo. He was a good boy. But what's *life* that you bring something *to* it, that's the irony . . ."

"Fill his glass," the host whispers.

"As if poor Yokoo is some sort of hologram—you know holograms?"

Nod. Of course a businessman knows holography, information storage and retrieval . . . but is he being goaded with his knowledge?

"Holography? yes, so we shoot our laser beams at him, Hey Presto, up he jumps, rescued from flatland. But what is more true art *this I ask you* my boy, information retrieval—or creation of it!"

Boiling a shade redder, ". . . which is most use to you, storing data or pulling it out again . . ."

"Exactly! Now you're catching on. An artist—or a businessman! Listen my boy while I read you this telex." Fumbling in his kimono sleeves, for a crumpled photostat. "ANTENNAE OF THIS MUL-

TICELLULAR ORGANISM HUMANITY PROBE THE ENVI-
RONMENT NOT SO MUCH TRANSMITTERS AS RECEIV-
ERS THE SENSUAL LABORATORY THE INSTITUTE OF
CONTEMPORARY ARCHAEOLOGY AND THE RANDOM
SAMPLES WE TAKE OF OUR ENVIRONMENT ARE DE-
VICES TO EXPAND OUR ABILITY TO ABSORB etcetera
etcetera SIGNED MARK BOYLE."

Urgent need to know, more Johnnie Walker.

"When did this message arrive?"

"Sixty years ago! I've had it up my sleeve since
then."

Head sunk in hand, to his wife's alarm. More
Johnnie Walker.

"Can't understand, can't understand, just a
businessman." Large tears, fat boiled out of his
face, sweat of panic as the stocks plunge.

"Art moves in cycles, hope you can ride one!"

"Do you mean . . . my Yokoos are done for?
Who's this Mark Boyle?"

"Forget about him, primitive level of technology. I guess he just sprayed plastic on the street
then peeled it off in squares and hung them up to
exhibit, but we can do something about his ideas
now, let me show you . . ." Fumbling in the huge
kimono sleeves again, knocking over the porcelain cup, which the wife swiftly sets up again and
tops up. Pushing a lobster still questing its antennae to one side, he places a red plastic box on the
lacquer table . . .

"It's a network, covers the whole city, they
beam arbitrary squares of environment, change
as often as you like, but one has no more value
than any other because they ALL have total
value."

Pressing a button, a square of fuzzy lines

springing up in front of the alcove where the girl poses in *The Gratitude of Aeschylus*, blotting her out, swimming into focus as . . .

a patch of gritty ground, some pebbles embedded, a used matchstick, a slurred footprint.

"Arbitrary art the art of true impermanence. . . because this site no longer exists in the same form, and the computer will never beam the same site twice. Twice unrecoverable, and that's what true art is—the unrecoverable moment. Mistake up till now has been to try to keep the supposedly significant moment alive for ever and ever, but look, this site is as significant as any other so it contains all significance, the same can be said of the next site . . ."

Johnnie Walker, stabbing the button again, *The Gratitude of Aeschylus* briefly visible, a new site hazing in, focussing . . .

a square of concrete with turd in one corner, grainy crumbling texture excretion of thick sand . . .

". . . changes the site automatically every 24 hours in case you get attached to it!"

. . . in place, on tiptoe in green fins, legs straddled, eyes wide open, seeing everything bathed in green by my contact lenses . . . not heeding the dinner party, WHERE IS IT?

So fashions change. Now it's my turn to join the Manet girls and Utamaro girls on the country fair and store roof circuit. My Master has put me out with the trash.

All the costumes and plastic figures to be sent to Dream Island our rubbish reef in the bay, and I am standing by them, free to claim them now they're trash . . .

But how much can I carry away—and where can I carry it to—and what's the use?

It's almost worth going to Dream Island myself. Why, I could live on the discarded food-gifts that pass direct from the Store to the Rubbish Island (almost) without any intervening stage of being opened by recipients (such is our wealth). Dress up in my roles against the backdrop of rubbish and feel at home—for I am rubbish now, in the eyes of fashion. A failure of nerve? Gradually allowing my poses to relax, moving a little at first, then a lot, till at last I was actually running about the island dressed as T's girls? Seems attractive—luridly attractive—but it wouldn't be my art as I know it—it might be something else, nearer to madness . . . Yet with more purity by far than the show booth or the store roof! I'd soon be respected by the outcasts—the other outcasts—who ferry the rubbish barges to and fro from the City, become maybe their Madonna, Mona Lisa, Angel, Onan Partner, in blue and red stockings with a pinned up skirt, hairy armpits and silver total-reflection contact-lenses. Set up the beachguard and the red devil with the flintlock musket and the wedding guest as if for gunnery practice on the hills of compressed cans and buildings of bottles, image sentries of our life. Straddle the plastic horseback with fish skeleton in my teeth. Bare my breasts and brush them with toothpaste peering through the smog for a vision of Mt. Fuji. The huge cut-out train in the oily surf lapping the metal rocks of the island, bearing me on its buffers waving the barges in with a giant plastic flower. Clipping on the tiny plastic breasts of Bardot I'd suckle the mice that scamper over the food-hills. With my striped sunshade by the striped water I'd wait for faceless people to admire me.

To live T's scenes at last in their totality!

The Grid moves over the City, at random, sectioning it into areas two meters square, beaming images of these to discerning homes where they are reproduced flat and vertical in the places of honor. Sectioned roofing, crowd heads, tire marks, footprints, flat spaces, rough spaces, rubble, hats, railway line, stone, glass, metal, turd. . . . The City can't be said to be dirty or clean, chaotic or ordered, natural or unnatural. Each two-meter section is what it is, includes all the others in itself, is part of TOTAL REALITY. The new art is popular with industrialists, the sanitation department, the town planners. The City cannot be spoiled ever again. The City IS. Its molecular geometry is innocent, elemental.

The Grid sections off the head and shoulders of a girl with total-reflection contact lenses in her weeping eyes reclining on a heap of crushed soft drink cans and cabbages traveling in a barge on a black greasy waterway. For 24 hours she halts in the grainy screening of the image, and hangs in the place of honor, till the computer selects another section at random, scuffed earth with a trail of impact craters arcing across it left by drops of dog piss.

But she is already on Dream Island, grinning, with her tongue sticking out.

OUR LOVES SO TRULY MERIDIONAL

Obi Nzekwu, age 35, profession: teacher of Geometrical Religion in a small school in Eastern Nigeria in the mid-Euro-Afro Conglomeration—that's me.

Till five years ago I was teaching common or garden geometry and algebra, there was nothing religious about Maths at all . . .

Then, need I say, the glassy Catastrophe Barriers appeared and we found the whole planet divided up neat as the segments of an orange. Bless Great Circle! Bless Greenwich Meridian! Bless Barrier!—we exclaim in joy.

It wasn't so much of a catastrophe for us, you see, as it must have been for those "less fortunately placed" . . . A euphemism, one doesn't speak in terms of "Elsewhere" nowadays, it's not done. (Non-names for non-existent places such as America, Australia, China and Japan. . . . !) The Education Ministry in Lagos has stopped issuing globes of the world with everything painted black apart from the single segment of the sphere that is mid-Euro-Afro. They're introducing a new design; the single segment alone. Visualize a bow with a fat bow-belly tapering to a point at top and bottom—a steel bow string taut between North and South. That's what the world looks like now, officially. (Besides, it uses less material, that way.)

And I have to teach this nonsense! I tell you, it offends me, logically!

We can see through the barriers, can't we? Eastward and Westward! Landscape doesn't just vanish into void. Or people. Or towns.

There's just no passing through physically. Or shouting with the voice. Or radioing. Aircraft that tried to fly over have slid to the ground in ruins. Nuclear missiles that the Euros tried to punch a hole through with went bang in the sky over the North Atlantic, but that was all. Tunnelling hasn't worked either. I'm not sure if wind and rain and such pass through—but I suppose they must, somehow, or there'd have been drastic climatic changes by now . . . which I haven't noticed. The Yam Rains have gone on falling at the right time for planting.

It's not actual glass. Though it looks like glass and feels like it to touch. Some force field, they say.

Of course being translucent we can read signs held up on the other side and talk in sign language—like bloody savages!—and I suppose theoretically news could be shuttled round the whole world from segment to segment by this mean. But it's discouraged, this contact thing. Irreligious, would you believe? By the time mid-Euro-Afro had banded together after the chaos and wars of the first two or three years, the pros-elytizing Church of Mathematical Geometry was in charge in most states of the Conglomeration.

Because, being "well-placed," we're quite

happy with the situation, would you believe?

We have to cross the Sahara to reach Euro, there's no sea route any more. But set against this, the Nigerian and Libyan oilfields; the industrial heartland of Euro; its best farmland; the forests of Scandinavia. All this in one unified Conglomeration! Then, politically, we Africans saw Namibia automatically liberated—and the remnant of White South Africa duly cut down to size! (The Catastrophe Barriers fell neatly into place on the Greenwich Meridian, then 20 degrees east of Greenwich, presumably following the same pattern all the way round and back again. From which you may deduce, if you like, that whatever put them there was perfectly familiar with our old way of mapping the world! I'd say at this point, consult a globe or an atlas, except that there aren't any, only under lock and key!)

Politically, the Euros are happy too. They can be friends with us, since the White Africa problem was solved by our Nigerian army in the first year. Then no more Soviet threat (for that matter, no more American imperialism!) and the inhabitants of the western sectors of Hungary, Poland and Czechoslovakia were delirious at their enforced separation from the USSR—even though they lost half their friends and kin in the process, and the tanks of the Soviet-Arab Alliance are parked up against the Barrier in plain view; another reason why we turn our heads the other way! Those may have wiped out the bulk of White Africa and earned our gratitude for it—but alas for Israel and so much else locked up in that segment! Much bloody chaos on our right-hand side, I assure you, which we learnt about from pathetic refugees clamoring up against the barriers with their signs like hitchhikers.

Our left-hand side was a sad case. England, sliced through Greenwich, with the East End of London included in our prosperous Conglomeration as a useless backwater town. The once powerful City of London itself in total decay, and the rest of the country a surly dictatorship obsessed with tilling the land. What else do they have in their segment? A few French fields, most of Spain, the poverty of Morocco, Mali, the Sahara . . . then northwards three quarters of Iceland, excluding Reykjavik: which must be almost totally isolated in a huge ocean along with a knob of Brazil. (I've scraped the blackout paint off an old globe to check—then hurriedly painted it back again.) Hard cheese, on our western flank! But we're doing very nicely, thank you, in mid-Euro-Afro. A heaven-sent blessing, the Barriers! So teach Mathematical Religion, count your blessings, don't squint east or west, pray the Barriers stay up. Don't ask who put them there. Say it was God. Or Allah. Or Forest Head. Some Alien Superbeing. Or even an all-too-human ABM Doomsday System. Paint the Globe black, except for your segment. Fine it down to a single steel bow-belly of a world.

THAT MIGHT BE ALL RIGHT FOR SOME PEOPLE!

All segments have to come together at the Poles. They must join together there. The Church has suppressed all mention of flights to the North or South Pole, to see. But there must have been flights. I'm highly suspicious about this silence.

So how about seeing for myself?

Not so impractical as it sounds. I can emigrate North. They need skilled labor in the Euro factories. Then, even if I have to hijack an airliner, we shall see what we shall see! Screw the Church, screw the Censorship. I'm for Truth. Me, Obi Nzekwu!

There must be others like me.

A tall Negro wearing a lightweight Euro-import suit that had come by lorry convoy all the way down the Sahara highway, with the segment emblem of the Church of Mathematical Geometry in his buttonhole, having thrown up his teaching post in the hot prosperous market city of Onitsha on the banks of the Niger, climbed aboard a lopsided mammy-wagon with the legend SEARCH YOUR SEGMENT FOR SUCCESS! painted along one side.

At Lagos he signed on with a Ruhr recruiting agency, receiving a one-way ticket to Euro in return.

The Caravelle flew due north across the great desert, the glass walls still hundreds of miles distant on either side, though he imagined them progressively narrowing the further they flew.

His seat neighbor was a Hausa similarly bound for a Euro factory, who confided that he had taught in Koranic School once. He too wore the segment emblem now.

"How could I go on bowing to Mecca?" he asked sadly. "Mecca is gone. The Kaaba, the Black Stone, is forever black and vanished."

"Maybe it's a test of faith?" suggested Obi buoyantly. "Besides, you never really bowed to

Mecca. Not accurately. Did you ever take the Earth's curvature into account? Your prayers were forever flying off at a tangent into space."

"In that case, maybe they were heard. By whoever it was. At least it has made the world a pleasanter place."

Obi was on the point of asking, "how do you know?" when he realized that for this man as for so many others the word *world* simply meant segment nowadays. Life was fine in mid-Euro-Afro so long as you didn't think of the exigencies to the westward, or the bloodshed to the east. . . .

I lost my love when the walls came down. He was left on one side, I was on the other. We'd even been holding hands a moment earlier. An inexorable force squeezed us apart. His hand became rubber then jelly and slid away to join the rest of his body *over there*. Let me remember this moment carefully. We were all taken by surprise. Taxis were crashing headlong into the sudden invisible obstruction. Such chaos and fire and broken vehicles and bodies. At first we all thought it was an earthquake. So we tend to forget certain things. Such as this very important fact: of what exactly happened to human beings such as Ichiro and I, who weren't riding taxis or trains but only standing quietly, a little apart, but in love, hands joined.

I felt a repulsion. Not emotional, but perhaps the sort of repulsion the butterfly feels for the chrysalis it separates from. Ichiro's hand seemed to become a pseudopodium—a protoplasmic tentacle thinning out and flowing back towards his body. A rope of cells. Then a string, a gossamer. Then nothing. Whereupon suddenly it was a proper human hand again, beating on the glass between us. I repeat, it's only an impression, this. Perhaps I was hysterical. So much noise and crashing of taxis and the suddenness of it! But I really think the Walls weren't designed to hurt us individually in the flesh if we were just standing about quietly, in love for instance.

I think of them as an experiment—a test, like an entrance examination. In my case, of Love. In other cases (there must be others), of human will, or dedication. Of the fine human qualities.

So, when we found we couldn't speak to each other, Ichiro and I, because this Wall was a wall of silence too, we scribbled characters in the air to make our minds clear to each other. Easy enough for us Japanese. We're used to misunderstandings, ambiguities in our words, that can only be cleared up by the invisible smoke signals of Chinese characters traced in a coffee bar, in the street, in a bus, upon thin air by our fingers . . . We vowed, by that means, to make our way to where the Wall ended, and be reunited.

It was to be our quest. There was some sense of *chivalry* about it, in spite of the burning taxis and the fires spreading to the wooden houses. We'd both been students of European Literature at the University, as well as lovers, and here was the impossible love quest given to us in the very heart of Greater Tokyo (strictly speaking, the petro-chemical-infested bay area—since the Wall came into being on the outskirts of industrial Funabashi). We seized this task gladly, as a gift!

I did, at least. I believed Ichiro. Alas—or is it really alas?—there's only the gift, the pure idea of the quest itself, to believe in, since he deserted me flimsily and callously after a few minor problems of travel arose, on his side . . .

Really, I don't care! I lost my love the day the Wall came down, but didn't lose Love itself. I am, like Marie-Henri Beyle (better known as Stendhal), "in love with Love." Someone will meet me where all the Walls meet. He will be the one who *deserves*.

Ichiro's excuses! Outside Otawara, our last meeting: the city on my side, paddy fields and vegetable patches on his . . . We stood on the useless rainway tracks, scribbling wisps of words in the air, and he said he was being drafted into the army. Did he mean the Self-Defense Force? No, he said Army and sounded proud of it, quite changed from his former pacifist self into an old-style classical soldier. What did he say all the young men were in the army for? A war between China and Russia, no less. Shanghai, Mukden, Changchun and Harbin, together with the North Koreans, were fighting an alliance of Seoul, Vladivostok, Manila and the Great Japan. He seemed to have fallen right back into the 1930s! Our own Japanese-Australian-Siberian Co-Prosperity Alliance is far more modern and civilized. I shrugged off his "patriotic" excuses, and hurried on north. We had the freedom to pursue our lives the way we wanted to in our democracy.

So I, Hiroko Chiyoda, had little difficulty making my way up the Narrow Road to the Deep

North, as did the poet Basho before me: through the Tohoku Region, across Hokkaido island, then on to Russian Sakhalin with its densely-wooded southlands and bleak northern tundra; thence by fishing boat across the Sea of Okhotsk to the city of Okhotsk itself (though Basho never came so far).

There in Okhotsk sadly I had to linger a long time working in a grim Russian beerhall (or *Peevnoy Bar* as they call them). Earning my living other ways too. Yet always thinking of Love, whatever! The War to our westward was followed by nuclear explosions in the Arctic Ocean. Maybe the Other Russians were trying to blast their way through the Wall in retreat? Nobody really knew. But as radioactivity spread through all the East Siberian Sea, travel was forbidden; and I would have to wait for the radiation to disperse before I went further north. I thought: if radiation can penetrate the Wall, so can the outpourings of Love! Over the next few years I almost became a native of Okhotsk, except that I never could forget the Stendhalian "pursuit of happiness". I, Japanese Hiroko, dwelling in Okhotsk among rough seamen, an amorous egoist biding my time, yearning for my soulmate . . .

After his year in the Ruhr factories producing machine tools, Obi Nzekwu succeeded in being transferred to the meteorological station on the island of Spitsbergen, thanks to his knowledge of trigonometry; and shivered through one long winter, till, on a late spring morning, as migrating birds settled down to land from Sweden and points south, he stole a plane equipped with skis instead of wheels and headed forbidden-north . . .

At last travel became possible again and Hiroko Chiyoda, through her connections with a certain Party dignitary in Okhotsk (and fluent now in Russian) became cateress on a Soviet icebreaker stationed, somewhat impotently, in the estuary of the Indigirka River facing Arctic waters. The *Marshal Grechko* was of the latest design (of seven years previous), with helicopter and spotter plane on board.

The Western War had seemingly ended in a stalemate, with Korea reunified from the North, the Chinese occupying the whole Khamorovsk area as far north as the Amur River, and Greater Japan helping the shattered Soviet hold the line to the north of them, while in the far south, with the help of the Darwin Australians, she was building overspill cities along the Timor Sea. (These suppositions she gleaned from her friend in the Party, just before joining the *Marshal Grechko*.)

Six months later, while they were cruising north of Faddeyev Island, having familiarized herself with the workings of a spotter plane and even flown out over the sea once with the Lieutenant-Navigator who'd become her new *ami*, she took off at dawn, alone, humming a lullaby about a cat.

The pursuit of happiness possessed her once more.

Something was black, at last, in the distance in all this white of ice. A spot, no more, at first, so that Obi rubbed his aching eyes doubtfully, afraid it

was an illusion brought about by staring too long.
Then he sensed the closing in of the great Barriers
on either side—sensed, more than saw, at first. Air
pressure rose sharply and there was sudden
turbulence—resistance, even, from the sky. Soon
auroral effects were visible in a V-shaped wedge
ahead, and he actually saw the translucent sky-
high walls tinted with a faint blush of rose, a hint
of violet, a cellophane amber. However the plane
was bucking and yawning too dangerously to
trust it any further. Taking a last hard look at the
(by now) black cone, he set his machine down on
to the snowfields, bumping and bouncing over
ridges to a halt. When he climbed out, he could
still see the cone, but illusion twisted it into a tiny
black man's face seen through the wrong end of a
telescope, set in an immense bundle of white
clothing. It wouldn't come clear. He couldn't
judge distance properly so that it could have been
any way away or any size. Besides, those auroras
were playing tricks with the periphery of his vision, spooks lurking in an invisible forest behind
glass trees whose height was awesome. He felt
scared, but set out, goggled and wrapped—the air
pressure mounting, forcing cold oxygen into his
lungs, that at least invigorated him.

Obi passed one ditched, abandoned airplane,
then another. Snow had drifted over them, hiding
them, and he wondered why it hadn't hidden that
black cone similarly. Scooping snow off the wing
of a plane, he watched it wander back along the
ground as though magnetized. How many ridges
and hummocks hid vehicles of one sort or
another, camouflaged by snow?

Doesn't the Polar ice-cap float on the sea beneath? Doesn't it swing round slowly? Shouldn't these planes have drifted south (for everywhere was south from here)—in some direction or other? Were the Barriers holding the ice-cap locked in place?

He wondered, but came up with no answers except that the black thing ahead must be the Alien Apparatus. The Doomsday Device. The Machine.

It was a full cone intruding upon all the Barriers.

Yet its base looked so irregular: indented and uneven.

Segmented too, a set of rough wedges arranged in a circle. The top half of a black fruit, broken up and put together again carelessly, with gaps.

A Machine?

Why not? Why assume that all machines have to be gleaming steel and aluminium?

But then Obi saw what the mound was.

Bodies.

Piled up fifty feet above the snow.

A separate wedge for each segment where the Barriers converged.

Bodies. That had scrambled over each other, to reach through and made a pyramid of themselves.

Bodies, which the snow left alone.

Obi touched one with his gloved hand. It came away covered with a fine black grit. The body was frozen hard. Even its clothes were sheets of steel. He tugged at it, to see its face, but it was too tightly locked to all the others that had climbed the slope before it—and, indeed, become the slope.

Cautiously, Hiroko set foot on the forty-five de-

gree incline of rigid, gritty corpses. Whatever fate
had overtaken them, she was sure would spare
her. The cone shape reminded her so strongly of
Mount Fuji, and even the black ash covering it
was so reminiscent of a miniature Fuji, that she
felt an instant surge of affinity with the mound, as
if it belonged to her, had been waiting for her
steps alone.

Something had electrocuted them. Something
had shocked them to death. Something that de-
posited this volcanic grit as a byproduct . . .

She climbed to the summit.

And there found a man whose face was black
standing looking at her.

She thought he'd just been killed—electrocuted, blackened—and hadn't fallen yet. Then he
grinned at her, and she realized that he was *Love*:
the black prince of her quest.

He said something. His lips moved but she
heard nothing. His hands gestured that he
couldn't hear her, either. Impatiently, both people
thrust their way into the final shimmery gap
where all the segments met.

She felt her shoulders pinched; had to turn
sideways, to force her way a little further. The
glassy walls pressed painfully on her chest and
back.

He too elbowed towards her strenuously, like
someone swimming through thick jelly. Reaching
out his hand to her.

Abruptly, briefly, both people seemed to become pseudopods—protoplasm flowing out, and
through each other's streams. There was a twisting lurch of the guts. An instant in which his heart
brushed hers, and their heartbeats meshed.

Then, a moment of discontinuity and she found herself standing with her back to him, staring down the far side of the cone.

At the same instant as Hiroko, Obi swung round crazily. Both stared horrified across the glassy gap that still separated them.

She started screaming at him. In Japanese, Russian, English, French. He howled English and Ibo and German at her. They only heard the noise of their own voices.

Already the walls were shimmering and squeezing at them. Air pressure became intolerable: an irresistible pillow forcing them back down the body mountain, to lose sight . . .

Obi ran far out on to the snow fields: far enough out to be able to see past the cone to the far side, where she should be by now. He halted, ice aching in his lungs. Only the cone and the white field round it were visible: no sign of any Japanese girl. He waited half an hour—an hour—till he had to walk away, or freeze.

He fled through the curiously magnetic snow, hunting for a buried airplane or snowmobile, wondering what segment of the world he was in now . . .

Hiroko had halted near the base of Mount Fuji. Taking her gloves off, she numbly fumbled a cigarette lighter from her pocket.

So electric, the air! So tinder dry! So combustible!

She flicked the lighter . . .

The Walls shimmered briefly—acquiescently, appreciatively.

IMMUNE DREAMS

Adrian Rosen returned from Thibaud's sleep laboratory with a stronger presentiment than ever that he was about to develop cancer. He wasn't so much anxious about this, as simply convinced of it as a truth—and certain, too, that in some as yet ill-defined way he was partly in control of these events about to take place inside his body . . .

"It's obsessional," Mary Strope grieved. "You're receding—from me—from reality. I wish you'd give up this line of research. This constant brooding is vile. It's ruining you."

"Maybe this recession into myself is one of the onset symptoms," Rosen meditated. "A psychological swabbing-down and anaesthetizing before the experience?" He lit another of the duty-free Gitanes he'd brought back from France and considered the burning tip. The smoke had no time to form shapes, today. It was torn away too quickly by the breeze, which seemed to be smoking the cigarette on his behalf—as though weather, landscape, and his own actions concurred perfectly. The hood was down, the car open to the sky.

They sat in silence and watched the gliders being launched off the hilltop, this red-haired, angular woman (fiery hair sprouting upon a gawky frame, like a match flaring) and the short burly man with heavy black-framed sunglasses clamped protectively to his face as though he had become fragile suddenly.

The ground fell away sharply before them, to reappear as the field-checked vale far below. The winch planted a hundred yards to their right whined as it dragged a glider towards it and lofted it into the upcurrents, to join two other gliders soaring a mile away among the wool-pack clouds. As the club's Land-Rover drove out from the control caravan to retrieve the fallen cable, Rosen stared at the directional landing arrows cut in the thin turf, exposing the dirty white chalk—in which the ancient horse, a few miles away, was also inscribed. Beyond, a bright orange wind-sock fluttered. Pointers . . .

"You don't even inhale," Mary snapped. "You could give up overnight if you were really worried."

"I know. But I won't. I'm seeing how near a certain precipice I can edge before . . . the lip gives way. It needn't be lung cancer, you know. It needn't have anything to do with cigarettes . . ."

How could he explain? His smoking was only metaphorical now. Cigarettes were a clock; a pacemaker of the impending catastrophe. In fact, he was fairly sure that it wouldn't be a smoker's cancer at all. But it sounded absurd whenever he tried to explain this.

Then, there were the dreams . . .

Rosen stood before the blackboard in the seminar

room of the Viral Cancer Research Unit attached
to St. David's Hospital and sketched the shape of
catastrophe upon it with a stick of squeaky chalk
that reminded him irresistibly of school days and
Algebra lessons . . . The difficulty he'd had at
first in comprehending x and a and b! His childish
belief that they must equal some real number—as
though it was all a secret code, and he the cryp-
tographer! But once presented as geometry,
mathematics had become crystal clear. He'd been
a visualizer all along . . .

On the blackboard was the cusp catastrophe of
René Thom's theorem: a cliff edge folding over,
then under itself, into an overhang impossible on
any world with gravity, before unfolding and flat-
tening out again on a lower level. The shape he'd
graphed was stable in two phases: its upper state,
and its lower state. But the sinusoidal involution
of the cliff would never allow a smooth transition
from the upper to the lower state; no smooth gradient of descent, in real terms. So there had to be
discontinuity between the top and the bottom
lines of the S he'd drawn—an abrupt flip from
State A to State B; and that was, mathematically
speaking, a "catastrophe."

(There is no gravity in dreams . . .)

He waved a cigarette at his colleagues: Mary
Strope, looking bewildered but defiant; Oliver
Hart wearing a supercilious expression; Senior
Consultant Daniel Geraghty looking frankly out-
raged.

"Taking the problem in its simplest mathematical form, is this a fair representation of the onset
of cancer?" Adrian demanded. "This abrupt dis-

continuity, here? Where we fall off the cliff—"

Rapping the blackboard, he tumbled Gitanes ash and chalk dust down the cliff. The obsession with this particular brand had taken hold of him even before his trip to France, and he'd borrowed so many packs from the smoking room downstairs (where a machine was busily puffing the fumes from a whole range of cigarettes into rats' lungs) that Dr. Geraghty complained he was sabotaging the tests and Oliver Hart suggested flippantly that Adrian should be sent to France *tout de suite*, Thibaud-wards, if only to satisfy his new craving . . .

"I suggest that, instead of a progressive gradient of insult to our metabolism, we abruptly flip from one mode to the other: from normal to malignant. Which is perfectly explicable, and predictable, using catastrophe theory. Now, the immune system shares one major formal similarity with the nervous system. It too observes and memorizes events. So if we view the mind—the superior system—as a mathematical network, could it predict the onset of cancer mathematically, *before* we reach the stage of an actual cellular event, from this catastrophe curve? I believe so."

He swivelled his fist abruptly so that the stick of chalk touched the blackboard, rather than the cigarette. Yet it still looked like the same white tube. Then he brought the chalk tip screeching from the cliff edge down to the valley floor.

Their eyes saw the soft cigarette make that squeal—a scream of softness. Adrian smiled, as his audience winced in surprise.

"But how can the mind voice its suspicions? I

suggest in dreams. What are dreams for, after all?"

"Data processing," replied Oliver Hart impatiently. "Sorting information from the day's events. Seeing if the basic programmes need modifying. That's generally agreed—"

"Ah, but Thibaud believes they are more."

Oliver Hart was dressed in a brash green suit; to Adrian he appeared not verdant and healthy, but coated in pond slime.

"For example, to quote my own case, I am approaching a cancer—"

Deftly, with slight of hand, Adrian slid the cigarette off the cliff edge this time, amused to see how his three listeners braced themselves for a repeat squeal, and shuddered when it didn't come.

"I shall have the posterior pons brain area removed in an operation. Then I can act out my dreams as the slope steepens towards catastrophe—"

Mary Strope caught her breath. She stared, horrified.

"Enough of this rubbish, man!" barked Geraghty. "If this is the effect Thibaud's notions have on you, I can only say your visit there was a disaster for the Unit. Would you kindly explain what twisted logic leads you to want part of your brain cut out like one of his damn cats? If you can!"

"If I can . . . No, I couldn't have it done in France itself," reflected Adrian obliquely. "Probably it'll have to be in Tangier. The laws are slacker there. Thibaud will see to the arrangements . . ."

Mary half rose, as though to beat sense into

Adrian; then sank back helplessly and began cry-
ing, as Geraghty bellowed:

"This is a disgrace! Don't you understand what
you're talking about any more, man? With that
part of the brain destroyed there'd be no cut-off in
signals to the muscles during your dreams. You'd
be the zombie of them! Sleepwalking may be
some temporary malfunction of the pons—well,
sleepwalking would be nothing to the aftermath
of such an operation! Frankly, I don't for one
instant believe Thibaud would dare carry it out on
a human being. That you even imagine he would
is a sorry reflection on your state of mind! Stop
snivelling, Mary!"

"Adrian's been overworking," whimpered
Mary apologetically, as though she was to blame
for his breakdown, whereas she had only been
offering love, sympathy, comradeship.

"Then he shall be suspended, pro tem. D'you
hear that, Rosen? No more waltzing off to France,
making fools of us."

"But I shan't be living long," Adrian said simply. "You forget the cancer—"

"So there, we have located it," Jean-Luc Thibaud
had declared proudly, "the mechanism that stops
nerve signals from the dream state being passed
on as commands to the body. Essentially the pons
is a binary switching device. The anterior part
signals that dreams may now take place, while the
posterior part blocks off dream signals to the muscles . . ."

Thibaud seemed a merry, pleasant enough fellow, with a twinkle in his eye and the habit of

raising his index finger to rub the side of his nose, as though bidding for cattle at some country auction. His father was a farmer, Adrian remembered him saying. And now his son farmed cats, not cattle.

"Thus we can remain relatively limp during our nightly dance with the instinctual genotype which psychologists so maladeptly label the unconscious mind . . ."

A hall of cats.

Each cat was confined in its own spacious pen, the floor marked off by a bold grid of black lines like graph paper. Lenses peered down, recording every movement the animals made on video tape.

Most cats were alseep, their eyes closed.

Most cats were also on the move. Scratching. Spitting. Arching their backs. Lapping the floor. Fleeing. Acting out their dreams in blind mute ritual dances of flight, rage, hunger, sexuality . . .

And a few, a very few, were only dozing, not dreaming. These didn't move. They hadn't drifted far enough down the sleep gradient yet. Soon they too would rise, and pace, and fight. Soon they too would lap the floor and flee. Till they dreamed themselves to death, from sheer exhaustion. It was tiring work, dreaming, down on Thibaud's cat farm.

From each cat's shaven skull a sheaf of wires extended to a hypermobile arm, lightly balanced as any stereo pick-up, relaying the electrical rhythms of the brain to be matched against this dream ballet taped by the video machines.

"And still I am dissatisfied, M'sieur Rosen!

Still, we see only the genetic messages for the most basic activities being reinforced. That's what this is, you realize? A genetic reinforcement. Errors creep in from one cell generation to the next. Too many errors, and—pouf! An error catastrophe. Death. So dreams strive to reinforce the purity of the genotype—like the athlete trying to keep himself fit by exercises. Dreams are error correction tapes manufactured out of each day's new experiences. But gradually we begin to dream out of the past, as the years go by. Increasingly we scavenge yesteryear. Soon, we are scavenging yesteryear's dreams themselves—using bygone, frayed correction tapes. We lose the capacity to make new ones. We dream vividly of childhood and it seems we are re-entering paradise as we sleep. Alas, that's all too true. We're about to leave the world, literally—for the cold clay of the cemetery."

"Yet I wonder, Dr. Thibaud, what if error is an essential part of our life process? What if, in order to be able to grow, we must also be able to die?"

"Yes indeed—the cruel dialectic of Nature!"

"Well then, what part has the cancer cell to play? It's the only truly immortal cell. It alone copies itself perfectly, without any error. And it kills us by doing so."

"The difference between cell replication and cell differentiation is a knife edge we must all balance on, M'sieur Rosen."

"Yet we all have cancer, potentially. Viral cancer lurks in everyone's cells in a latent form, did you know? I want to know why. Doctors perpetually set themselves up to cure cancer—to cure polio, to cure everything else they label as disease. And that's supposed to be the whole work of medicine. But how many doctors ever trouble to glance at the whole system of life and evolution that a 'disease' functions in? None whatever!"

A cat— a mangy, skinny alley-tabby—pounced on the invisible prey that it had been wriggling its way towards all the time they talked. But almost at once it leapt away again. Its fur stood on end, its tail bushed out, as it backed cowering into the corner of its pen.

"Did you see that, M'sieur Rosen? You could call it a catastrophe, in your terms—that sudden switch from fight to flight. The mouse becoming a monster in its mind. Yet how much do we really see? It's as you say about medicine—scratching the surface. Examining the arc of the circle and thinking that's all there is to the figure! But the inner landscape of the dream must be just as important as the actions. If not more so! In fact, I'm inclined to think the full subtleties of the genotype can only be coded into the dream as environment. Yet how to show that? Still, we're only starting on our journey inwards. Come, see the darkroom. We raise some other cats in black light and isolation from birth, so that they display the perfect archetype of a dream . . ."

The alley-tabby awoke, as they retraced their steps, and whined from the fretful exhaustion of having slept.

"Presumably, in an archetypal setting . . ."

Their glider bounded over the turf as the winch

driver heeded the blinking of the aldis lamp from the control caravan, then slid smoothly into the air, climbing gently towards and upward of the winchgear. Mary pulled back softly on the stick, increasing the angle of climb to balance the downpull of the cable, till at eighty degrees to the winch and an altitude of a thousand feet she dipped the nose briefly, pushed the cable release knob, then climbed away.

"What if it doesn't let go?"

"It disconnects automatically, if you're at a right angle to the winch—which you shouldn't let happen."

"It could jam."

"There's a weak link in the chain, Adrian. By design. It's fail-safe." But she sounded exasperated.

The hill upcurrent sent the glider climbing towards scattered woolly cumulus in a sky which was the blue of a pack of French cigarettes, as Mary manipulated the controls efficiently, banking, centralizing and taking off rudder, then repeating the same turning maneuver with a minimum of slip and skid. And so they spiralled aloft.

Her hair blazed back in the wind when the glider did slip to the right briefly on one turn, uncovering the firm rhombus of her cheek-bones, and a number of small brown moles just in front of the hair line. For a redhead her skin was only lightly freckled. It resembled the grain of an old photograph more than distinct freckles. Adrian loved touching and stroking those few hidden blemishes when they were in bed together, but it

generally took a strong wind to whip the bonfire
of hair back from them.

"So you're set on going to France?" she said at
last. "I think Geraghty would rather Oliver went."

"Oliver doesn't have my special interest."

"What interest? It's nonsense!"

"You know very well."

"I know nothing of the sort! You're perfectly
healthy. Why else do you refuse to take a medical?
It would show how wrong you are."

"I can . . . examine myself. The dreams, you
see. It would spoil everything to have some silly
check-up. It would ruin the experience. I must
keep perfectly clear and neutral."

The glider skidded badly then, as Mary angrily
used a bootful of rudder, and the nose began hunting, pitching to and fro.

"You realize you're wrecking our relationship?
Your scientific credibility too! If that matters to
you!"

"My dreams have a shape to them. I have to . . .
live them out."

Correcting the trim of the machine, Mary spiralled the glider through the wool-pack, avoiding
entering cloud. They soared above the snow cocoons into open sky; the clouds swept by below
them now like detergent froth on rivers of the
air—the vale and Downs being the soft clefted
base of this surge of translucent streams. They
continued a stable upward helix for another few
hundred feet till uplift weakened and Mary
swung the machine away towards a thermal bubble on which another pilot was rising a mile away,
in company with dark specks of swifts and swal-

lows catching the insects borne up along with the
air.

But if they'd entered cloud, reflected Adrian,
and if another pilot had also done so, and the
curves of the two gliders intersected in the wooly
fog, then there'd have been . . . discontinuity: a
catastrophe curve.

Marguerite Ponty accepted the infra-red goggles
back from Thibaud and Rosen to hang on the hook
outside the second of two doors labelled DEFENSE
D'ECLAIRAGE!

The slim woman's dark glossy eyes were heavily accented by violet eye shadow which made
huge pools of them; as though, having spent too
many hours in null-light conditions tending to
the darkroom cats, her senses were starting to
adapt.

Her hair was short and spiky, gamine-style. She
wore dirty plimsolls, blue jeans and a raggy
sweater under her white labcoat, the loops of the
knitting pulled and unravelled by cats' claws.
From her ears hung magnificent golden Aztec
pyramids of ear-rings. Her scent was a strange mix
of patchouli and cat urine: clotted sweetness and
gruelly tartness grating piquantly together.

"The pons area is lesioned at one year old,"
Thibaud commented. "They've never seen anything. Never met any other cat but their mother.
Yet in their dreams they prowl the same basic
genetic landscape. The computer tells us how
they show the same choreography—only pur-
ified, abstracted. What is it, I wonder? A Paul
Klee universe? A Kandinsky cosmos? Has anyone
unwittingly painted the genetic ikons?"

"Let's hope not Mondrian," laughed Marguerite. "What a bore!"

"Blind people dream," Rosen reminded him. "Surely they don't visualize. They smell, they hear, they touch."

"And out of this construct their landscape, yes. Same thing. It's the putting together that matters. The shaping."

"Topology."

"Exactly. I was only using a metaphor. Let me use another: our blacklight cats are dancing to the same tune as our sighted tribe. Yet they experience next to nothing in their lives."

Rosen couldn't help glancing pointedly at Marguerite Ponty's looped and ragged sweater. They experienced her.

"Which proves that dreams are control tapes for the genes, not ways of processing our daily lives. But come. It is time to show you our cancer ward. We use nitrosoethylurea to induce tumors of the nervous system—thus the immune battle is fought out within the memory network itself! The basic instinctive drives yield right of way to a more urgent metabolic problem. You'll see the shape of catastrophe danced. That's what you came for."

Rosen grinned.

"Immune dreams, yes. But what landscape do they dance them in?"

"Ah, there you ask the vital question."

Another day. Another flight. Another landing. And Rosen had been to France, by now.

Mary pointed the glider down steeply towards the two giant chalk arrows cut in the field.

It struck him that she was diving too steeply;
but not so, apparently, for she raised the nose
smartly to bring them out of the dive flying level a
few feet above the ground, the first arrow passing
underneath them, then the second. They slowed
as she closed the airbrakes, pulling the stick right
back to keep the nose level, till they practically
hovered to a touchdown so perfect that there
was no perceptible transition between sky and
ground. She threw the airbrakes fully open, and
they were simply stationary.

Cursorily she rearranged her hair.

"Nature's so bloody conservative," Adrian persisted. "It has to be, damn it, or there wouldn't be
any Nature! You can't have constant random mutations of the genotype. Or you'd always be losing
on the swings what you won on the roundabouts.
So once a particular coding gets fixed, it's locked
rigidly in place. All the code shifts that have led
from the first cells through to cabbages and kings,
have operated upon redundant DNA, not the main
genome. Look around, Mary. How diverse it all
seems! Sheep. Grass. Birds, insects, ourselves. So
much variety. Yet genetically speaking it's almost
an illusion. Quality control is too strict for it to be
any other way. Just think of the Histone IV gene
for DNA protein-binding. That's undergone
hardly any change since people and vegetables
had a common ancestor a billion and a half years
ago. Biological conservatism, that's the trick! But
what's the most conservative cell we know?"

"Cancer, I suppose," admitted Mary. "What are
you driving at now?"

"Quality control to the nth degree!" he rhapsodized. "That's cancer. And now we know there's viral cancer lying latent in everyone's cells. It's part of our genetic inheritance. Why, I ask you?"

"To warn the immune system," Mary replied brightly. "When a cell goes cancerous, the virus has a chance to show its true colors as an alien. Our immune system couldn't possibly recognize cancer as hostile tissue otherwise."

"Very plausible! Then why's the system so damned inefficient, if we've got these built-in alarms? Why do so many people still die of cancer? Have medical researchers ever asked that, eh? Of course not! They never think about the whole system of life, only about correcting its supposed flaws."

"Maybe more cancers get stopped early on than we realize?"

Adrian laughed.

"So you think we may be having low-level cancer attacks all the time—as often as we catch a cold? There's an idea! But I fancy that viral cancer's not locked up in our cells to warn the immune system at all. The reason's quite different. And it's so obvious I'm surprised no one's thought of it. Cancer's there to control the quality of replication of the genotype—because cancer's the perfect replicator."

"That's preposterous!"

"Cancer isn't the alien enemy we think. It's an old, old friend. Part of the Grand Conservative Administration presiding over our whole genetic inheritance, keeping it intact! It's a bloody-minded administration, I'll grant you that. It has to be, to keep in power for a billion years and more. Thibaud was fascinated when I outlined my theory. It casts a whole new light on his genetic dream idea—particularly on the class we're calling 'immune dreams'. Cancer's catastrophe for the individual, right enough. But for the species it's the staff of life."

"Your health," Thibaud grinned broadly: a farmer clinching a cattle deal. Marguerite Ponty smiled more dryly as she raised her glass, clicking her fingernails against it in lieu of touching glasses. Her earpieces shone in the neon light, priestess-like. Were they genuine gold? Probably. Her joke about Mondrian referred to her father's private collection, it transpired. Rich bourgeois gamine that she was, she'd chosen the role of a latterday Madame Curie of the dream lab— as someone else might have become a Party member, rather than a party-goer. There was something cruelly self-centered in the way she regarded Rosen now. Of the two, Thibaud was much more vulgarly persuasive . . .

Thibaud also looked genuinely embarrassed about the wording of his toast when the words caught up with him.

"A figure of speech," he mumbled. "Sorry."

"It doesn't matter," said Rosen. "It's the logic of life—the cruel dialectic, as you say. Thesis: gene fixation. Antithesis: gene diversification. Synthesis: *ma santé*—the sanity of my body, my cancer."

"Yours is such a remarkable offer," Thibaud blustered, beaming absurd, anxious goodwill. "You say that an English specialist has already confirmed your condition?"

"Of course," Rosen produced the case notes and passed them over. He'd experienced no difficulty forging them. It was his field after all. And if Thibaud suspects anything odd, thought Adrian, odds are he's only too willing to be fooled . . .

Still, Thibaud spent an unconscionably long time studying the file; till Marguerite Ponty began flicking her gold earpieces impatiently, and tapping her foot. Then Rosen understood who had paid for much of Thibaud's video tape equipment and computer time. He and the woman regarded one another briefly, eye to eye, knowingly and ruthlessly. Finally, hesitantly, Thibaud raised the subject of the clinic in Morocco.

"It will take a little time to arrange. Are you sure you have time—to revisit England before you come back here?"

"Certainly," nodded Rosen. "I need to explain some more details of the theory to my colleagues. The cancer isn't terminal yet. I have at least two months . . ."

They sat in Mary's convertible, watching other gliders being winched into the air: close enough to receive a friendly wave from one of the pilots, with whom Mary had been out to dinner lately. A surveyor or estate agent or some such. Adrian hadn't paid much attention when she told him.

Or was he a chartered accountant?

The winch hummed like a swarm of bees, tugging the man up and launching him over the vale. Geologically speaking you'd classify it as a "mature" valley. In a few more tens of thousands of years, weather action would have mellowed it beyond the point where gliders could usefully take advantage of its contours. But at this point in time there was still a well-defined edge: enough to cut the vale off from the hill, discontinuing, then resuming as the landscape below.

Mary lounged in the passenger seat. She was letting Adrian drive the car today. It was the least she could do, to show some residual confidence—since Geraghty's suspension of him; though it was some while since they'd actually been up in a glider together.

Softly, without her noticing, he reached down and released the handbrake.

Once she realized the car was moving of its own volition towards the edge, he trapped her hands and held them.

"Look," he whispered urgently, "the genetic landscape."

"Adrian! This isn't a dream, you fool. You aren't asleep!"

"That's what they always say in dreams, Mary."

He pinned her back in her seat quite easily with dreamlike elastic strength while she cursed and fought him—plainly a dream creature.

Soon the ground leapt away from the car's tires; and he could twist round to stare back at the face of the hill.

As he'd suspected, it betrayed the infolded overhang of catastrophe. The shape of a letter S. Naturally no one could freewheel down such a hill. . . .

Later, he woke briefly in hospital, his head turbaned in bandages, as seemed only reasonable after an operation to excise the posterior pons area of the brain. He found himself hooked up to rather more equipment than he'd bargained for: catheters, intravenous tubing, wires and gauges proliferating wildly round him.

He stared at all this surgical paraphernalia, curiously paralyzed. Funny that he couldn't seem to move any part of him.

The nurse sitting by his bedside had jet-black hair, brown skin, dark eyes. He couldn't see her nose and mouth properly—a yashmak-like mask hid the lower part of her face. She was obviously an Arab girl. What else?

He shut his eyes again, and found himself dreaming: of scrambling up a cliff-face only to slide down again from the overhang. Scrambling and sliding. A spider in a brandy glass.

MY SOUL SWIMS IN A GOLDFISH BOWL

This terrible cough. It tears me apart every morning when I rise, like a dawn wind: the cold of morning meeting the warmth of the night and sucking it out of me. That's the picture I have of it, as though I'm sleeping in some yak tent on the high steppes somewhere, not in a town flat. It's been happening for over a week now: ten, fifteen minutes of convulsive, hacking strain; irritating to Mary, who thinks it's deliberate, a mannerism, a parody of middle years, a protest. It's all dry; nothing comes of it.

The Doctor tapped my chest last night, harkened to his stethoscope, peered down my throat. Nothing. Congestion? Something stuck in my windpipe? No. Tonsillitis? No. Digestive troubles, tickling the coughing reflex misleadingly? None that I've noticed. He has me booked for an X-ray, but the possibility remains, as Mary believes: habit spasm, hysteria. Myself doing it. To protest at something in our lives, in my life.

So it comes. In the bathroom, the awful hurricane from within. And I grip the firm white washbasin with both hands, as lungs implode and eyes bulge, as I shed tears of blood (so I fancy). Will I burst a blood vessel this time? Will I have a heart attack?

And at last, *at last*, this morning I do cough up something. Something quite large. Rotund, the size of a thumb nail. It lies squirming on the white enamel. Phlegm alive.

What is it? I wonder in disgust as the tears clear. Part of my lung? A living gob of lung, still breathing the air—fresher air out here than in my chest? It pulses gently, wobbles, throbs. It's alive. What on earth is it?

A cancer, a tumorous growth, still growing fresh cells, unaware that it has lost its host? Some other unknown parasite that has been living in me? Surely no such thing is known. Look, it still quivers with undoubted independent life.

An abortion, a thumbnail foetus has erupted not from the womb (which obviously I don't have) but from my chest, and rests there, still alive. Some spirit of sickness, finally exorcised, which my bloodshot overstrained eyes somehow perceive—in the style of some juju witchdoctor who spies out the soul of the disease. The Philippine faith healers supposedly pull impossibilities, nodules, out of the body to cure it . . . Have I, then, become a healer *in extremis*? Can I march up to sick people now, plunge my hand into their bellies and chests and tubes, and haul out their diseases, alive and squirming? I prod it with my finger. Wormlike, it contracts, bulging another way. Yes, it's a living being—or antibeing. Dare I wash it away? Or should I shuffle it into a matchbox, keep it prisoner?

I tap the plug in the sink, wash warm water in—and it floats, swims around like a sluggish tadpole.

"Mary! Come and see! I've coughed something up. It's alive."

She comes to the bathroom, then, and peers into the bowl.

"Can you see it, Mary? Here!" I poke it, and it tumbles over in the warm water, rights itself. "You do see it, don't you? Say you do. It came out of me just now. It lives."

"Oh I can see it."

"Maybe that's the spirit of the sickness. I've coughed it out at last?"

"It isn't that, Tom." She backs off, her expression diffident. "Don't you realize? It's your soul. You've lost your soul."

"My . . . soul? You're joking! How can it be my soul?"

She retreats from me. Detaches herself. The bathroom is very white and clean and clinical, like a surgery. The thing in the sink circles, executes a flip.

"What else can it be, Tom? What else lives in you? What else could you lose?" She peers at me. "You're soulless now. The soul's quite a little thing, you see. It hides inside everyone. Nobody ever finds it, it's a master of disguise. It doesn't have to be all together so long as its atoms are spread out around the body in the right order, one in this cell, one in that. But yours has clotted together, it's condensed itself—and you've just ejected it. Lost it."

"But," I poke the thing gingerly, "what gives you such certainty? Such conviction!"

"You don't feel certainty any more? That's because you've lost the thing that gives conviction, faith, belief. *I know*. Because I still have mine, spread throughout the whole of me. But yours has been narrowing and congealing for months now. It went from your lips, your heart, your fingers. It went from your eyes, from your belly, from your penis. It's been retreating, pulling in on itself all these months. I know,dear."

"Supposing," I grip the bowl, "for the sake of argument this is my soul, do I scoop it up and gulp it down? Do I get it back inside me that way?"

The living object somersaults, ducks under water, surfaces lazily. It seems to have no particular sense organs or organs of any sort or limbs. It's all just one and the same thing. A living blob. Does it eat? Does it absorb energy?

"Can I reincorporate it?"

"Unlikely. It's too dense now. You'd only eat it, dissolve it in your stomach acids, excrete it out. Parents lose their children, mothers lose their babies from their wombs, you've lost your . . . Well," she shrugs, "it's gone its own way now, Tom. It's outside you."

"Is this some cruel joke of yours? Do you really hate me so much? Have you been hating me all these years without telling me?"

"Hatred, dear, doesn't apply if the soul is gone; nor love. Besides, how could I possibly love or hate *that*? But life goes on, obviously. You'll have to look after it, Tom."

We have what used to be, once, a goldfish bowl on top of the drinks cabinet in the dining space; now a flower bowl with a posy of anemones, artificial ones of silk. The goldfish died after a few months. Of loneliness perhaps—if a fish can feel lonely. Of emptiness, and the horror of the empty world being so bent round upon itself. I can't very well flush my soul down the drain, like an abortion, can I? Even if there's only the merest suspicion that it really is my soul. So I take the bowl, laying the posy on the dining table—then rush back in panic in case Mary pulls one on me. My soul's still there. Mary's back in the bedroom, humming, putting on makeup. I scoop my soul carefully into the bowl, add more water, remove it to the safety of the drinks cabinet beside the little drum of daphnae, undiscarded year in year out. Do I feed it on daphnae? It appears not to possess a mouth.

"Mary—I've put it in the bowl. Please be careful, won't you? God, the time! Do I go to work on the day I lost my soul?"

"Don't worry, Tom, it'll be safe. Today's like any other. Better than a pet rock, isn't it—a pet soul?"

A pet. But it looks nothing like a pet, any more than an amoeba could be a pet. There it is, a huge amoeba, afloat, semimobile, doing its own thing oblivious of me. Goodbye, Soul, for now; I'll be home at six. Don't get bored, don't do anything I wouldn't do.

It circles, rotates, pulses a bit.

Mary will get her hair done, then pick up the food and wine for the meal tonight; Tony and Wanda Fitzgerald are coming round. Brittany artichokes, steak and strawberries, I suppose.

So off to work I go. While my soul stays at home.

If Mary put the bowl on the cooker and heated the water up, I wonder would I feel the searing pains of being burnt alive? Agonies at a distance? I should have found a better place for the anemones.

However, no such agonies arrive. Indeed, all day long as I examine my sensations, I feel very little sensation indeed. I coast in neutral. Things get done. I entertain a client to lunch; does he notice that my soul is absent? Apparently not. I wonder whether other people really have souls at all—perhaps I was the only one? After lunch I call in on impulse at a church. I ring the confessional bell, I pull the curtain. This is how I believe one goes about it. I've no practical experience of such things.

"Yes, my son?"

"Father, I'm sorry but I don't know the right routines. The formulas. What one does. I've never been in a confessional before—"

"If you suddenly feel the call, plainly there's a need. What is it?"

"Father, I've lost my soul."

"No soul is ever lost to God, my son."

"Mine is lost. To me. Well, not exactly lost. No—I still have it in a sense, only it's not in me any more—"

Useless. I stumble out.

Work.

Home.

Mary's hair is exquisite, if over-precise. I smell the tarragon in the Breton sauce prepared for the artichoke leaves, and hurry to the drinks cabinet, heart thumping, absurdly fearful that my living soul is chopped into the sauce with the tarragon leaves. So vulnerable I feel with my soul detached from me; yet at the same time curiously I feel very little about it . . . But no. My soul still circles slowly there, aloofly. I prod it. It ducks, bobs up again, like jelly.

Tony and Wanda arrive. I pour gins and whiskies.

"Whatever's that?" asks Wanda, pointing.

Mary smiles brightly. "Oh that's Tom's soul."

Everyone giggles, even me.

We sit down. We eat, we drink. Conversation does its glassy best to glitter. Smoke fills the air. Mary places the bowl with my soul in it on the dining table as we drink coffee and some odd beetroot liqueur from Rumania. My soul circulates. Tony offers it a stuffed olive on a skewer, the olive being the same size as it is. It butts against it, declines the offering; how could it nibble it? When Tony withdraws the olive I look twice to ensure that by some slight of hand he has not exchanged my soul on a skewer for an olive bobbing in the bowl. But all is well.

"It really is his soul, you know," says Mary. "But don't imagine it feeds or thinks or does very much! It's just something that *is*."

"An essence. How existential," nods Tony. After a while my soul is relegated to the top of the cabinet again. Where it rotates, quite slowly, mutely in its bowl.

After a while longer its presence seems to overcast the evening; Tony and Wanda leave rather early, murmuring excuses. It's disconcerting to see someone's soul, looking just like that and no more. If only it was radiant, with wings! A hummingbird. A butterfly . . . But it isn't, alas. This miracle, this atrocity, this terrible event is too small and simply protoplasmic, too tadpolelike. Where is the amazement? Where is the awful revelation of loss? And this is why I know now, with absolute certainty, that my soul does indeed swim there in the bowl. Lost to me utterly; so utterly that not even a thread of awe or a spider's strand of sickness unto death can connect me to it.

Such is the nature of real loss, irreparable total loss; no possible attachment remains. So it is true that I am soulless; for there it is. Just that and no more.

While Mary rinses plates, I sit patiently watching it as it turns, and turns, limbless, eyeless, brainless, mouthless, turning nevertheless, occasionally ducking and bobbing in its tepid water in the bowl.

My soul, oh my soul.

THE ROENTGEN REFUGEES

Auroras flickered overhead: dancing spooks tricked out in rose and violet and orange veils, only vaguely held at bay by the daylight, returning every night in their full . . . should one say glory?—yes, it was glorious . . . or rage?—yes, it had been rageful. Every night, sheets of mocking pseudoflame put all but the brightest stars to flight, preluding that not so distant day of the Nebulosity when the whole visible universe might be reduced to a few dozen light years in volume and the art of astronomy die, except for chance glimpses through vents in the swirling skirts of thin, bright gases.

They rode a military halftrack driven by a soldier called Kruger, hosted by the vulgar Major Woltjer.

"Did not ought to have been Sirius!" Woltjer glared over his shoulder at the four passengers, accusing them of incompetence—though they weren't astronomers or physicists.

"This here is Smitsdorp Farm we're moving onto now." His eyes lingered on Andrea Diversley—pressed too tight up against the Indian geneticist, with her arm round his waist. Such shameless affront to his Afrikaner principles in the presence of other whites! His gaze raped and whipped the Englishwoman for it. Yet apartheid was such an unimportant thing nowadays, when you came to think of it!

"Did not ought to have been! What do you think, Miss Diversley?"

"True, Major, the Dog Star played a dog's trick on us."

"Well, did it not so?"

Smitsdorp Farm seemed to be recovering its grass cover adequately by contrast with barrens they'd passed. Far too adequately perhaps, here and there. These patches would have to be looked at later—and the soil, the grubs, the insects, the micro-organisms. Right now, their route was towards the low hills where some of the irradiated seeds that had been stored in the open and sown in control strips had produced some exceptionally high yields, but might be genetically unstable or even nutritionally undesirable.

Woltjer tried his best to shame her into untwining from the Indian; but she only shrugged.

"It isn't my field of study, Major."

Tired of twisting his neck round, he stared ahead over the rolling ravaged acres of a farm that would never support grazing herds again.

"Scientists!" he snapped.

So what did he mean by that? wondered Simeon Merrick, who was sitting behind Andrea and her Indian next to the taciturn, defensively chauvinistic Swede, Gunnar Marholm. That scientists of any breed whatever bore some responsibility for events in the interior of the Dog Star?

Disaster. Yes. But amazingly, in the event, it

hadn't been Mankind's doing. After so much scaremongering about nuclear warfare, the running down of resources, overpopulation and pollution—all kinds of doom sketched out for the nineteen eighties—disaster, when it had come (as everyone obscurely sensed it must: that was one constant in everyone's calculations), came wholly unpredictably, from a source wholly external to Mankind's affairs.

Yet how could it be external? Was it not an illusion to think of it as external?

What hath Man wrought, that God in his Wisdom should permit—no, engineer!—this cosmic event? That He should so dislocate the order of the heavens and the order of life on Earth?

What hath Man wrought, ten years ago, that should finally tip the scales of God's estimation? Simeon hunted back through the decade before for some exemplary evil—that eluded him.

What earthly events could have prompted the terrible explosion of the Dog Star, as absurdly shocking to the astronomers as it was to this Afrikaner soldier Woltjer? What sequence of sins? Perhaps simply too many people had stopped believing in God?

Ridiculous! No single event or set of events could decide God's mind. (Yet, recall the Cities of the Plain, Simeon, remember Sodom and Gomorrah! Those had reached a crucial point, attained a critical mass of sinfulness—they had gone too far!)

Surely the modern God was no such petty dictator, petulantly setting fire to a star to scourge his sons and daughters?

It just had to be the whole trend of human history; of accumulated sin. Sins such as South Africa itself. Sins of exploitation and segregation. And yet, and yet, fretted Simeon, wherefore Dear Lord Thy choice of this special moment in time? And why wasn't it the Whites who had died? Why wasn't it the rich and powerful who perished? Why was it the Blacks, the Browns and Yellows? The poor, the wretched of the Earth. Why was it they who disappeared? Why was it the Major Woltjers of this world who came through—going down the deep mines which their wealth came from, for the first time in their lives, and sheltering there, while above ground the black miners took the peak dose of 8,500 roentgens, and died? The same pattern was repeated all over the globe. The embarrassing querulous voices of underdevelopment were stilled forever. It was the developed peoples of the world who had the resources and the technology to survive. The "Cleansing Operation" he'd heard the supernova referred to in Jo'burg by men like Woltjer. Cleansing operation. All political and moral embarrassments cleared away by the charged particles that followed on the heels of that flare of light, which itself gave only the briefest months of warning.

The Clean Up. Why?

And still Woltjer was angry at Andrea's tenderness to this Indian, who'd had the impertinence to survive, and who now accepted these white liberal caresses with such greedy nonchalance.

"Did not ought to have been!"

"No, indeed," Gunnar Marholm said brusquely, to silence him. "It did not, but it was. So are we to blame, somehow? Is science? Don't you know that it all happened several times before in Earth's history? Look in the geological record, man! You'll find mass exterminations of fauna there. A probably acute dose of 500 roentgens every 300 million years. A single dose as high as 25,000 roentgens once since pre-Cambrian times. Agreed, it was an unfortunate star to explode. Being so near us. Giving such a high peak dosage."

Simeon looked out of the window at the recuperating earth. The blessed sight of renewed chlorophyll. But amongst and around, lay a hundred skeletons of cattle, tattered hide still clinging on white bones.

And scattered among them were human skeletons. Kruger drove the halftrack right over them, making no effort to detour.

"The universe doesn't owe us a living, Major," murmured the Swede.

Yet how the Lord had helped those who helped themselves! Oh yes indeed, those who had helped themselves to the fruits of the earth all along had had their great granaries to hide in from His wrath—and hide successfully they did! Sweden had done all right out of the Clean Up too, with over ninety per cent of her population saved. Not that Sweden, to be fair, could be accused of having "helped itself" compared with the other developed countries. The record was honorable. Was this why Gunnar Marholm acted so icily chauvinistic? wondered Simeon. Because he felt his own people's survival to be tainted by that of the real pirates of the globe, who weathered the

storm a shade less successfully than social demo-
cratic Sweden, to a lesser degree of antiseptic
perfection? Yet still magisterially successful beside India, with only one half of one per cent of
her people saved; or Nigeria, with one tenth of one
per cent! Britain, prime ex-colonist, saved 52 per
cent. American saved 54 per cent, mainly whites.
While this South Africa they were now riding
through scored 80 per cent—all of them Whites
since no non-White was considered to be a South
African, by definition.

The Swedes, after all, were Whites. They were
whitewashed with the same brush as Britain,
America, Germany and France.

The Lord helps those who help themselves. The
meek and the poor are burnt like chaff.

Is God then illogical? Inconsistent? Yet surely it
couldn't be that it had nothing to do with God?
From this thought Simeon recoiled. God could
neither overlook, nor could He commit illogic or
evil. There must be a Purpose.

One half of one per cent: no, India hadn't done
at all well. Thus the caresses of the English woman, guilt that could only assuage itself by her
surrender to Dr. Subbaiah Sharma as slave to his
erotic demands . . .

"Geological record, Gunnar?" argued Simeon,
worried and upset—while the halftrack crunched
over the bones of those Zulu or Xhosa people.
"The only comparable event we really know is the
Bethlehem supernova—the star of the Magi
which God kindled to tell us of the coming of his
Son. Now there comes this second."

"This second what? Second Coming? Ha! A

random accident. Let it have happened fifty years ago and only the merest remnant of the human race would have pulled through, if any. As it is—"

"Yes?" cried Andrea, hugging Dr. Sharma to her, twisting the knife in her conscience. "And as it is?"

"As it is," shrugged Marholm—for they had been through the argument before, "assuredly hundreds of millions survived. Maybe as many as five hundred million. The populations of the developed countries, by and large . . .

"All the statistics aren't in," he reminded her.

Sharma laughed. His presence: a walking corpse's, a ghost's—a living reminder of the forever dispossessed.

"It seems that the meek haven't inherited the earth after all, as your Bible promised, except as this bonemeal around us!"

Andrea hugged him, loving him for the whole abruptly terminated agony of underdevelopment. She herself had weathered the cosmic storm down in Goblin's Pit near Bath, in the Wansdyke Commercial Deposit, as a Priority A Survivor, class of Agricultural Botanist.

"But hell," blurted Woltjer, just when it seemed the matter was losing its momentum, "it did come as a kind of blessing, let's be honest. I mean, population problem's solved! We don't need to worry about squeezing ourselves off the planet. Using up all our resources. See what I mean?"

"Oh yes," cried Sharma. "Yes I do see, Sir. Was it not generous of us three billion people to move aside out of your way?"

Thought Simeon: he identifies himself as a

corpse, yet his erotic clamorings nightly deny this—unless we regard it as a form of necrophilia in reverse.

"Oh Subby! Please!"

But oh, how the mere presence of the Indian scientist spelt imperfection and untidiness in a God-given clearance programme, to Major Woltjer's mind!

"Many more creatures besides us colored people need not feel guilty at taking up room any more!" And oh, how he was exploiting Andrea. "Such as all large mammels—a good thing, Major? Byebye elephants, giraffes and camels. Byebye whales and seals and dolphins. Byebye crows and eagles, doves and hawks. Byebye byebye."

Lord God, Who in Thy mercy didst send the plagues upon Egypt to save Thy people, did You also send this plague from the Dog Star to save Your people—that this human race might not entirely destroy itself by its own hand, as seemed so very likely, and thus rob Thy Earth of its fairest crown of creation? Too soon, Dear Lord, too soon, to terminate Thy plan?

"Second Deliverance? Second Bethlehem?" Simeon murmured the words aloud; and Subbaiah Sharma greedily battened on them.

"Those that have, shall have more, Simeon. That is the new Bible. Those that have little, shall have nothing. Even the dignity of burial is denied them."

The halftrack crushed another African skeleton. Many lay bunched about here—like a migration. A resumption of the Bantu migrations of old.

Woltjer merely smirked. "God helps those that help themselves."

They passed through heaps of dry bones which the new grass was forcing between: a thousand cattle skeletons, a thousand human skeletons. Though we drive through the valley of dry bones, let us fear no evil, prayed Simeon to God, Who must know.

Anonymous bonemeal in rags and tatters of cast-off European garments.

"They did not ought to be in this zone!" grumbled Woltjer. "Wasn't authorized for Bantu, you know, hereabouts. Silly Kafirs must have thought they could make the jump on us when we evacuated."

"Maybe their only remaining dignity," the Indian said quietly, "was to be walking across this land that was once theirs, when the roentgen storms arrived. To die saying: this is our land after all, and you can't ever take it from us again. Because now there's nobody to take it away from!"

"You can see the cultivations ahead," Kruger pointed.

As they worked among the queerly prolific corn and mealies and sorghum, Woltjer strode about kicking the occasional bone. Kruger left his driver's seat, approaching Andrea and Sharma with a leer on his face.

"You think there'll be mutations? You think there's mutations in insects and things? Read about mutants in a book once. What monsters there might be after an atomic war. What miscegenations."

Sharma eyed him distastefully. "But it wasn't a nuclear war, Sir. So no radioactive isotopes lie around. The radioactivity of isotopes made by cosmic rays is a very secondary matter. There shan't be any monsters breeding to roam the earth."

"Is that so?"

"Sorry, nothing so interesting. Just a kill-off process. Most exposed fauna. From now on it will be a world of very little things—and Man. Man will be big and overwhelming. Otherwise, insects and micro-organisms and of course some fish in the sea. But mainly man: six foot tall man towering over it all. Seeds are highly radio-resistant, so man will manage to feed himself cereals and vegetables. A vegetarian world at last! A few million more people will die before enough food is available. In the more impoverished countries, needless to say."

"That so?"

"Then Western Man will have the planet to himself. European Man. Man of the Future. What a rich technological civilization he will enjoy in another few decades, when all this unpleasantness is no longer remembered—no more social irritants or aberrations to disturb the order of things!"

"Don't, Subby. Don't demean yourself talking to him. You're worth ten Afrikaners."

Petulantly Sharma shook off Andrea's hand.

"Ten Indians and a dog! A westerner's dog used to eat ten Indians' food, did you know? I wonder how many dogs and cats were saved in the shelters of the West?"

"There were rules, Subby. They were strict. But there had to be some kind of Noah's Ark operation."

"Ha, ha."

"For chickens and pigs and such. If only to restock. We must have some animal protein."

"How many Indians was an English pig worth? Or an English chicken?"

"But we lost our people too, Subby!"

"Yes, your Indians and West Indians. How careless of you."

"We lost white people too."

He shrugged. "The working class."

Andrea turned back to her botany. Her eyes seemed moist but Simeon couldn't be certain, for just then Kruger let out a shout of surprise and sprinted back to the halftrack. He brought a couple of rifles with telescopic sights and tossed one to Woltjer.

Simeon stared at the hills, shading his eyes against the bright sun—and shading his mind against those dancing veils of heaven high above the fleeting cottonball clouds.

He saw a ragged column of raggy people trekking down from the direction of Broederskop, led by a tall bearded white man carrying a red and white flag flying from a gilded Latin cross.

As they came closer Simeon worked out the design of the flag. It was a white skull on a blood-red background.

Alpha Canis Majoris A, Sirius the Dog Star—an energy spendthrift not quite nine light years distant from the Earth, twice as massive as the Sun and twenty-five times as bright, though only one third as dense, and hardly a candidate for supernova status judged by its place in the Hertzsprung-Russell diagram—exploded nevertheless, discharging between 10^{49} and 10^{50} ergs as cosmic rays, producing a massive flux at the top of the Earth's atmosphere and a worldwide radiation dosage at sea-level, over a three day period, peaking at 8,500 roentgens—where the normal natural background dosage is only 0.03 roentgens per year . . .

Three billion human beings died as a consequence. Those who were unsheltered.

Most birds and beasts and shallow-water fishes died.

Most flora was defoliated (but would recuperate asexually or through seeds and spores).

The sky flamed rose and green and violet with charged particles trapped in Earth's magnetic field. The sky had never been more beautiful.

However, few stood up to praise the glory in the sky.

In a million years, the reason why would appear in the record of the rocks . . .

"I thought you didn't grant shelter to any Africans, Major?" said Sharma innocently.

"Africans? What Africans? We are the Africans. Is what Afrikaner means! Bantu, is what you mean."

"The terminology of a twisted mind."

"No, it is accurate. We was here first, before the Bantu."

"And you're still here, after them?"

"Damn right!"

Woltjer gripped the rifle tighter, squinting through the sights.

"You're not just going to shoot, for no reason?"

"Naw, Miss Diversley. I'm looking at them. But they're crossing a non-permitted zone, those Bantu."

"A what?" cackled Sharma. "You must be mad!"

"Unless they are servants or hired labor with passes."

"Oh fine—that lets me in! I qualify as hired labor, don't I? Thank you for reassuring me, Major."

"Subby—!"

"Yes, all right Andrea." Yes, it would be all right for Subby later on, thought Simeon, with a smirk of the mind which he couldn't quite control. Subby would sublimate his racial humiliations later on. Feeling ashamed of himself, Simeon caught a fold of flesh between his fingers and pinched hard till it ached.

"Unh, I know the fellow with the flag, Frensch is his name, was a pastor. I thought he'd have died; must have found shelter. Wonder where he's been the past year?

"Kaffir-lover," the Major added.

"It looks like they plan on coming on down through the plantings, Major."

"So I see, Mr. Marholm. Spoil the plantings. Trample our food with their dirty feet."

Woltjer swung his rifle away from the column and fired off a shot. It crashed horridly, leaving a silence of deafness behind it. Andrea covered her ears, bottling up the sound of the gunshot in her head.

Marholm laid a calming hand on Woltjer's arm.

"I'm a good shot, don't worry. I aim to miss. Send them round the plantings. Just looking now. Watching."

The column did veer away, to angle round one corner of the plantings.

"Good enough," grunted Woltjer, lowering his rifle. "I recognize one of the Bantu. Name of Stephen Ambola. Had trouble with him. Not a political extremist exactly. A religious agitator, like Alice Lenshina. Remember her Native African Church?"

The gilded cross, the white skull flag, tottered round the perimeter of the cultivated area and headed their way again.

At first, the column struck Simeon as a parody of nineteenth century explorations of Africa with its white leader bearing aloft the symbol of empire, pursued by a gang of skinny black bodies. Then his vision readjusted and the troop was . . . a wretched medieval crusade. Not of knights and squires, but of starving people. Of diseased people, burning with blind faith. It belonged in the corner of some medieval horror by Hieronymous Bosch. A children's crusade. A crusade of innocents and wretched.

"What you want?" bellowed Woltjer. "I know you, Frensch, what you doing here?"

The bearded man handed the cross and flag to the African behind him, who gripped it with fierce determination and rammed it into the soil.

Most of his followers squatted down exhausted. Stephen Ambola and Frensch approached.

"Put those damn guns away. Who do you want to kill? We're not going to attack you."

"Bantu shouldn't be on this land. Government Experimental Farm. Can't risk trampling the crops with their dirty feet. Get them off, Frensch."

"What does it matter?" cried Ambola. "Old feuds! Forget them. We have the News. Don't we?" He turned to Frensch.

"As though it wasn't staring us right in the face!" Frensch raked over a human skull with his boot, then gestured vaguely and derisively at the veils of color flickering above the scudding clouds.

"News? What news?" Anxiety gripped Simeon. He could be tipped any way in his beliefs, out in this vale of bones, in the face of this raggy anachronistic band of people. Fanatics. Yes indeed. But had they thought out any better explanation than himself? Or than the Pope, whom the bulk of masonry over the Vatican's vaults had sheltered with his College of Cardinals and a mass of faithful, from the roentgen storm?

The Papal Encyclical *In Hoc Tempore Mortis*, issued three months afterwards, had been a temporizing rather than a mortifying document. It injected placid placebos into an implacable situation. Pious wishes for the success of the Food and Agriculture Organization and other world agencies. It was a programme for survival—while the whole theological dilemma remained unsolved: the why and wherefore of God's permitting only one tenth of His flock, principally the one tenth that was white and rich, to survive, when nine tenths of the meek and humble perished. The why and wherefore of His refashioning the Eye of the Needle so that the rich merchants could pass through, replete with bag and baggage, leaving the starving hordes to perish outside the city walls.

This skinny African in torn shirt and broken plastic flipflop sandals, with burning intelligent eyes, stared into Simeon's face.

"I bring news for those smug in their survival!" he sang. "They did not survive. They've been damned by God. Same as you, same as us. Every man, woman and child alive on Earth today are the damned souls. God took the blessed and left the damned behind. He was merciful: He saved *so many*. All that He could save. But He couldn't save all and still be the Just God. Those who live today are those he couldn't redeem in any way. Any way at all."

"Shut your mouth, Ambola," Woltjer snapped. But Ambola would not and did not.

"Who are *you* Damned Souls?"

Andrea Diversley's voice begged:

"We're a team from the Food and Agriculture Organization of the United Nations."

"So South Africa's in the UN these days? Don't miracles just happen? All the miracles of Hell!"

"We're botanists, we're plant geneticists. The irradiated seeds . . ."

"Ha! Cultivating the plains of Hell. Wasting your time, pretty woman."

Woltjer struck out wildly at Ambola with his gun, but Ambola had already skipped out of the way.

"Apologies, baas. I forgot Hell still has its policemen."

"I became aware of the News, you see, Damned People," Frensch interrupted. "Blessed souls in the skies—*look at them*. You see them even in daylight." His finger jerked up, pointing beyond the cottonball clouds at those fearful veils of glory.

"Yes," Simeon whispered, horrified. "I do see now."

"Simeon! What are you saying?"

"But I do see, Gunnar. The Pope was wrong. *In Hoc Tempore Mortis*—so inadequate. Though we walk through the valley of the shadow of death . . ."

"Don't you see, Damned Man, we walk through the valley of the shadow of life! That life of souls up there. Blessed life casts the shadow of its glory on us here below."

"So charged particles are souls, are they?" The Swede laughed scornfully. "Now I've heard everything. You could expect messianic cults to spring up like weeds in these circumstances, Simeon—but my friend, we've got a big job to do."

Frensch faced the Swede squarely. "This is no Messiah cult, Damned Man. For there never will be any Messiah. The Messiah, He has come and chosen and gone. Left us behind Him. Yet the authority of His church still stands—there's no reason to doubt our faith. Only, our faith is not now in salvation but damnation. A Church of the Abandonment. The bleached skull flying from the cross. So we must go forth to waken people—so smug in their survifal, when they have already been weighed in the balance and found wanting."

"A Church of the Abandonment—yes, that fits," murmured Simeon. "Otherwise, God would have acted illogically. He would be unjust. And that can't be."

Frensch stepped forward and grasped Simeon by the shoulder.

"Welcome to Damnation, Damned Friend. Help spread this news. We must move on to the towns and other lands now—to tell the Damned of their Damnation."

"Simeon!" the Swede begged. "This is more ridiculous than any of the guilty contortions Andrea performs."

The Englishwoman darted him a poison glance, moving closer to the Indian geneticist till her body was brushing his.

"It was just a natural disaster, don't you see?" soothed Gunnar. "As has happened before. As happened to the dinosaurs. Yet we can understand and mold our fate, unlike the great reptiles! That is our humanity."

Shaking his head, Simeon refused to understand.

These petty scratchings in the earth's devastation that the new plantings were . . . in a vale of dry bones, while the wretched and the meek had all been taken away into Heaven—to become those dancing ghostly veils of beauty high above the clouds. That symbol of Damnation planted in the crumbling soil: the gilded wooden cross with the breeze fluttering out from it, the white skull against the red of Hell's spiritual fires which burn but consume not . . . And oh, the ragged, fervent survivors—these Crusaders!

It was the last crusade of all: a crusade of total faith and total despair.

Woltjer shook his head stupidly as though his ears were full of water. He brandished his rifle; he blustered. No one paid much attention.

Andrea twined her arms round the Indian's neck, kissing him furiously before the gaze of Africans and Afrikaners.

Gunnar Marholm had retreated into a cold northern fastness of the mind, blankly gazing across the African soil at the glint of white bones.

Above the clouds, danced a rainbow joy of colors.

There was such silence, but for the faint sigh of wind. No birds or beasts anywhere.

"Did not ought to have been Sirius," blustered Major Woltjer, squinting round him, useless rifle at the ready, where no threat loomed. The silence gulped his words down as a cow a fly.

The Church of the Abandonment squatted silently, eating or resting.

Frensch and Ambola went back to their standard and rested by it.

After a while Simeon walked over too, and sat under it.

There was the wind.

And the wild veils aflame in the sky, violet and green and rose.

And the emptiness of the earth.

A TIME-SPAN TO CONJURE WITH

Disconcertingly, only one small township was visible on the entire planet's surface, though forty years had passed since we first set down the colonists. Even this we had to hunt for by heat-scan for quite a long time before we could locate it optically, because—even more disconcertingly—it was situated defensively at the very heart of the largest continent, almost as though they expected ravenous beasts to crawl out of the sea, sending long tentacles squirming far inland.

When the colony had been founded forty years earlier—eight years by our ship's calendar—it had been set on the shore of a bland and fruitful ocean. We expected to find a thriving port and harbor on our return, with sea links through the chains of islands to the minor continents, and a rather slower opening up of the vast empty interior—sending out feelers around the indigenous primitives without disrupting them. Instead of which, the colony had crawled inland—as far inland as it could get . . .

Yet it could hardly be tidal waves they feared, as the world was particularly unseismic: unmountain, unrifted, a world of gentle prairie where the merest pimple of a butte was a major landmark; nor tides either, as there were only two diminutive moons, each barely larger than our own starship.

"Crawled is the word," I remarked to Commander Marinetti, as we at last watched a telescope blow-up of the only town—while Resnick vainly tried to raise some kind of radio response from the colonists. "They must have dragged it here by hand!"

There was the peculiar crawling over itself of the finished product, too. Various mini-suburbs seemed to be trying to arrive at the same central downtown spot, whilst still hugging the ground as closely as possible, rejecting the skyscraper or pyramid form as a solution. Low, flat buildings were plugged together (out of the original clip-together prefabricated modules of the once-neat harber township, apparently) in higgledy-pig-gledy "sheets" like a round plateful of jostling, overlapping sandwiches. The concentric chaos bore no relation whatever to the neat formal grid and broad avenues of the coastal town we'd helped them build.

"I suppose it is a human town?" Marinetti hazarded. "The primitives couldn't have supplanted our colonists, I don't suppose?"

Hardly. The primitives had been a shy, and shying lot. Melting away into the merest dip of the prairies, behind a blade of grass almost, when we tried to contact them. We never saw much of them, no matter how long we flittered about the interior. Only traces, tracks, occasional fleeting ghosts in the corner of your eye, gone by the time you turned to stare. Difficult to describe them!

Fey ghosts. Flitting fairies. Puckish "human" dragonflies. Any of these. All of these. They seemed insectoid with their (apparently) multi-faceted eyes, flightless gossamer-winged thin arms, wasp-waists, thin banded furry legs—a provisional taxonomy pieced together with enough difficulty, almost entirely out of the corner of one's eye! Trip cameras invariably flashed their photos, and wasted them, just as the subject was stepping into view; just the moment before He/She/It appeared before the lens.

The natives seemed closer to nature than culture; still at a level of pre-understanding. They made fire (somehow). We found the char marks. They cooked small game and birds that they (somehow) caught. We found the bones, sucked clean, though no traps or nets, unless some pieces of string wound from grass qualified. No arrows, darts or spears, certainly, though a few thorns stuck into pieces of stick. But on balance we felt they weren't really advanced enough for us to disturb their fleeting, evasive way of life inside their continent, any more than a man camping on the edge of a huge field influences the moths and butterflies in it; unless he sprays them with insecticide, of course—and that certainly wasn't the intention! So, for a plus, there would be no pathetic, broken aboriginals begging for crumbs from the technologically rich man's table; no ruined native culture whose Gods had arrived and stolen their dreams away. For a minus, of course, they were simply uninteresting. We'd left it to the colonists themselves to find out more, eventually. It wasn't a priority—then. We expected better things—more amazing, more assertive beings elsewhere.

"A disease hit our people, and the natives inherited our bits and pieces?"

"They couldn't even lift the bits, never mind plug them together," I pointed out.

"Well, why's it there, in the dead center of nothing? Instead of, oh, harbors, docks, island-hopping townships . . . ! They were going to leave the interior free. Just in case, for the natives. But that's exactly where they expanded to! Only they haven't even expanded, they've contracted there."

"Something unexpected in the sea? From the sea?"

"Oh, come. You'd hardly need to put a thousand kilometers of land between yourself and it, whatever it was!"

"Maybe the sea itself is alive, in some strange way, with algae as its nerve cells? Maybe after a while it realized and radiated hostility at the human intruders?" I romanced—almost hopefully.

Marinetti laughed.

"Like you, I'd love to meet the utterly exotic for once! I have the same hunger for it, my friend. But it was a fairly normal ocean—just somewhat saltier and distinctly richer in fishes than any ocean we've seen since." A note of bitterness crept in.

True, alas. In all our years of flight the stars had turned out to be rather ordinary; so far we were the most surprising feature. Of the five "live" worlds suitable for colonies, only this one, the first, bore anything at all complex: the Fairy Aboriginals.

The other live worlds were at an early Paleozoic stage: ranging from a serene extreme to a wild, convulsive volcanic extreme. In one way this was delightful, for it meant we had the whole worlds to ourselves, with atmospheres and water, albeit somewhat deficient in humus and vegetation. (But that could be dealt with.) Each could be developed—uniquely, wonderfully.

In another way, this became increasingly depressing as the years went by, while colonists slept and we stayed awake, exploring, exploring. We found nothing, except what we had been sent out to discover: fresh worlds for human colonies. Nothing astounding, nothing special. Here we were, returning to Earth via the first world we had settled, with absolutely the dullest, emptiest landscape of all—though it did have its birds and small beasts and "Fairies", at any rate!—returning to see what humanity had brought in forty years activity; and perhaps, just perhaps, to find that something interesting had been gleaned—just a little would do—about those natives we had dismissed (though not derisively or destructively) as butterflies and moths, while we pressed on to greater things. Humanity would thrive and expand because of our efforts; but we were disappointed men and women.

And now, what price our colonizing effort even—and Earth's huge outlay—if forty years had only served to produce this puny settlement in the middle of undeveloped nowhere?

"Maybe the boredom of the landscape . . . unstimulating?"

"Maybe the absence of tides—?" Marinetti and I

had the same idea at once. Different ends of the same idea.

"A bad prognosis for the other worlds?" he hinted.

"Those volcanos on Hekla should keep our people on their toes," said Resnick brightly. We'd named our newfound worlds Cambria, Hekla, Livingstone and Zoe. The one now below us was called Haven, betokening the hope of a sea-borne culture, as well as our first port of call. Properly we should have called some world "New Earth". It was expected; we knew that. However, it had turned out that the only world we could honestly have used the name for was Haven; and by then we had passed up the chance, as Haven seemed altogether too monotonous and blank for such an honor. So now we were taking the name back with us, unused. And our colonists, likewise had hardly used their Haven at all; but only taken refuge deep inside it. Against no visible storm whatever.

The next day we detached the smaller survey craft from the bedstead-like assemblage of *Starseeder* (progressively dismantled and disencumbered of its luggage sufficient to furnish five worlds, till it was a mere stargoing gridwork returning home) and dropped down towards the town, Laura Philipson piloting, to land a hundred meters from its outskirts (crawling over its inner skirts rather like flattened tortoises attempting glacial copulation).

It was indeed built from exactly the same permaplastic modules which had once been set out so neatly by the shore. Some embarrassingly primitive mud and wattle additions had been made round the extremities. Very little indeed achieved, beyond the huge ridiculous endeavor of hauling the whole settlement a thousand kilometers inland . . .

Fields of Earth vegetables grew around the town. There were irrigation ponds and ditches. All looked well enough tended outside the town perimeter. On the other hand, otherwise they would have starved. Puny agriculture, though! Puny.

Maybe you couldn't give a proper head start to a colony on an alien world if it was ever really to be their own world? Maybe a colony had to sink down to the lowest cultural level before it could start to climb, of its own accord, to "civilization"? Some unknown social law? Was this what had moved them to haul everything as far away from their starting point as possible?

Fairies were flitting in the fields. Now-you-see-them-now-you-don'ts.

However, there were humans too. Twenty or thirty people appeared from a narrow alleyway between the modules.

They hardly swarmed out to mob us. They just stood waiting patiently by the buildings. And so we walked between a field of cabbages and a field of beet, to greet them instead. (While a fairy appeared and disappeared behind a monstrous, healthy cabbage.)

I recognized the original leader of the settlement, considerably aged, not surprisingly. A man named . . . Greenberg, yes. Greenberg had been a tough stallion once; now he looked a tired work-horse . . . My God, what had happened to their *animals*? Their horses, sheep and cattle? That original stock of embryos, brought starward frozen in rabbits' wombs, should have multiplied a hundredfold by now; where were they?

And their children?

Where were their children? I saw two or three men and women in their early forties who must have been born during the first year or so of settlement. No one any younger though. And a huge age gap between these few "youngsters" and all the other oldsters.

Bad. Dreadful. The worst.

Their fertility had been blocked. And the fertility of their animals. What by? By the sea breeze? By some undetected chemical which took several years to reach a critical level . . .

"No children or animals."

Marinetti nodded. To the small reception party, he announced:

"Well, we've come back. We've settled four other worlds successfully—" He talked a little while, a little floridly and formally, trying to make theirs seem a dignified defeat, I suppose. Greenberg and the others only stared at us, as though from the other side of aquarium glass. When they finally responded, it was shiftily, awkwardly, irrelevantly; impatiently, as though there was something we really needed to know, and dismissively, as though they cared not a hoot. More "Fairies" flickered in the fields. For the first time I caught a proper glimpse of one, and was surprised to see that the diaphanous insect-being—and others, and others!—seemed to be actively tending the crops, here and there, in a sort of erratic, fanciful Brownian-movement way. The creatures were almost perfectly camouflaged by their near-transparency, presenting bodies as a kind of thin, vibrating grid over the scenery, which one tended not to notice head on, only picking up their movements laterally.

"But haven't you any children?" Marinetti was repeating for the third or fourth time. Greenberg gestured at the fields.

"Children?" he smirked. "Children have to be taught their lessons."

"Do you mean they're in school? *Where are they, man?* Why are you all living here out among the natives?"

"Taught, for instance," proclaimed Greenberg, "that the sun draws light into itself; or that a pebble draws ripples to itself from across a pond. Taught to see such things."

They hadn't merely gone infertile, they had gone crazy—with grief at the absence of children . . . ?

Marinetti let our small party be led—hand in hand with the colonists, as though otherwise we might stumble or walk into walls!—down that poky alley between the clipped-together modules with their mud and wattle additions—which I suddenly fancied were not for the human beings at all, but represented their idea of what Fairy folk might like to roost in: a lure for Fairies, architectural equivalent of a dish of milk set down to gratify a household imp!

They had deliberately come into their midst.

None of the colonists bothered carrying any weapons. Had they taken the evanescent Fairies for the only "Children" they could ever have?

We arrived where the outer "suburb" block made an effort to climb over the inner ring; from this point we had to walk over the roofs of the inner modules for a little way till a wooden ramp took us back down to ground level, along another alley debouching into a small "park" at the center of town, with a dirty village pond. A few more souls joined the little crowd escorting us: all in their early or late seventies. Hardly a dangerous or inclement world, I reflected. Just, that they had failed to breed. Just, that they had gone, collectively and pathetically, silly. Even the younger people, the very few in their forties, were just as "senile": rambling, forgetful, assertive, fussy— their minds motheaten tape-loops. Quite a few other people didn't even bother approaching us, though they must have known who we were. They just went about their own business, oblivious to us. Incredible.

A bowl of pebbles stood beside the filthy pond. With a practised "ritual" gesture Greenberg picked out a pebble and tossed it into the pond. Plop. The ripples spread out, rebounding from the edge. Greenberg stood for a while, admiring the patterns, then urgently he rushed us inside a module with the faded stencil legend, AD-MINISTRATION, still on it. Just at the moment of going in, I glanced at the roof, attracted by a faint flurry of light. As though called by the "plop" of water, one of the Fairy folk had arrived, overhead, racing—flying?—over the rooftops. It flickered briefly then was gone again.

Inside an empty room, on an otherwise bare table, stood a tumbler of clean water, with a black pebble floating incongruously just under the surface.

The pebble dissolved. It began diffusing through the water, in coils and clouds of . . . no, it hadn't been a pebble, but a large blob of ink—a blob of ink which began to mix with the water but which certainly had not been mixing *till* we walked in! There had been no one else in the room before us. No other doors led from the room; the window and skylight were bolted shut.

Marinetti stared at the tumbler, perplexed. Greenberg picked it up, shook it from side to side, emphasizing the inevitable mixing of ink and water, then set it down heavily.

"Did you see that?" he leered.

A blob of ink had "unmixed" back into the same blob it had once been—by chance, at random, the moment we walked in? Then started to mix again? Out of all the billions of molecules of ink, out of all the billions of molecules of water, out of all the positions they could be in, they had suddenly reverted to their original unmixed state? But it would take thousands of billions of years for such a thing to happen by chance, if indeed it could be encompassed within the lifespan of the universe. That we should walk in upon it—and Greenberg react as though he expected it? Didn't the Second Law of Thermodynamics apply here? Were there supposed to be different natural laws for different worlds?

"Oh, no" I protested quickly. "Somebody *prepared* that just before we got here! Or *something* did," I added, remembering the flicker of light on the roof.

"We thought of that explanation," remarked Greenberg.

"One of those Fairy creatures! Hypnosis. Or psychokinesis. Some mental force you don't know about—"

"They help with the crops. They have a beneficial influence. We love them; they may as well be our own children—" He smiled benignly.

"But they're sabotaging the colony. They must be."

"And yet, the truth is we are *their* children. . . ." Then—as though the sight of the inky water discharged some kind of static from Greenberg's brain (murk into murk, as it were) the man became lucid and began to talk coherently at last, approximately on our wavelength; a mental cripple, briefly peering through the bars of his disorder into the real world once again, struggling to communicate his disorder. "It's their sense of time . . . Odd to us. Real for this world. The appropriate *Umwelt*. The right perceived environment. The successful evolutionary one. The sun draws light into it, the pebble draws ripples to it: that's the way *we* see it, I don't say that's how it is. Though we're learning. Such a strain and a nuisance, having to talk to you like this, explaining. We've adapted well, considering. We're used to living here. It wasn't unpleasant, once we got right amongst them. It was so disturbing and tormenting, before that—until we got here and adjusted. Two or three years, lost out there by the sea. It took another two or three years trekking, to find the right spot—the place of power. But we're catching on now—"

"You aren't *adapting*, man! You're dying out."

Snatching up the tumbler of inky water angrily, I rushed out of doors and jerked the contents violently into the pond. I heard Greenberg's laughter behind me, from the doorway. He came out and removed the empty tumbler from my hand, bent down and refilled it with murky water, which he took indoors and set on the table again. A rite. a rite of murk and water. The impossible separation, the reversal of the flow of time. Automatically, I glanced at the roof. There was no sign of any Fairy there now. I felt annoyed at myself for looking; then enraged that creatures so insubstantial, so evanescent, had apparently caused so much harm. They weren't fairies, they were devils. But how had they done it? Thank God that Cambria, Hekla, Livingstone and Zoe had been such raw, dormant worlds, after all, with no mischievous higher life!

"Those creatures are obviously responsible," nodded Marinetti. "But what are they? I can hardly see the damned things."

"After a few years, you cotton on," confided Greenberg. "They're a superior adaptation, no doubt about it. We'd have broken down but for their guidance . . . Signs, such as the de-inking of water."

"In what way superior?"

"I mean more widespread than us—"

"Since you haven't bred yourselves, nor bred your animals, but only shrunk to this pitiful muskox-at-bay circle in the middle of nowhere, that must be the case!"

"Not widespread in that sense." Greenberg struggled to express himself. "Not in your sense. I guess it's hard to remember that you yourselves can't see how they've spread out around you, the way we can now."

Greenberg braced himself; from now on he talked in a stiffly lucid way, with a huge, resentful effort, like someone having to speak in a foreign language they despised.

"They're not widespread in the sense of numbers. They're spread out in time, do you see . . . *In time*. No, you can't see, that's the whole trouble. Not till you learn the trick. I guess that's why they have those faceted eyes, so they can perceive the different present moments . . . different quanta of the present. Listen, Mister Starship Commander with your clever Einsteinian time dilation, I tell you they can perceive duration, the way you perceive extension in space. Imagine yourself always looking at the world through a narrow tube. Things will seem to be appearing and disappearing all the time, while you look around, right? But actually the world stays linked up and constant, because we perceive extension. A frog doesn't see the world our way, though. It just sees a few patterns and movements. If a thing keeps still, it's just *not there*. Bits of the real world just aren't there at all! We're better than frogs, because the world's all here for us all the time. But *how much better are we, eh?*"

"You're not saying that we're like frogs, compared to these Fairies?"

"Oh, I am! They live in a world, as large again! They perceive *duration*—extension in time. That's the world they live in!"

"Fairyland!"

"So you only see them a little, every now and then. Yes, we're like frogs, only seeing the fly when it moves. Not seeing all the world that's really there. How can we possibly influence or exploit a world we can't see? It isn't like our not seeing X-rays or radio waves yet still being able to build sensors to detect them . . . We can't build sensors to *see* duration. How to? The concepts don't exist, for Men—"

"They certainly seem to exist for you!"

"Oh, we're being shown. We're learning. We're not really their children. More like their pets. Their experiment. We're more convenient to them here, than at the coast, you see."

"Why didn't you *stay* there?"

"Couldn't," mumbled Greenberg angrily. "The . . . pressure of their *Umwelt* . . . the suction towards the center of the land . . . too much. The whirlpool of their sense of time . . . intruding on us. You'll understand, if you stay a few years. How is it now? You feel the world enduring moment by moment: one moment after another. The past, fixed, gone forever. The future, just about to happen. In between, there's the specious present: how long does it last? How much present-time do you feel you inhabit? Something between three and seven minutes, I'd say. That's about the length of time you feel the 'present' lasts, isn't it?

Well, how long is their present? It's hours—days!"

"You mean they see into the future?"

"No! Their present is *larger*, that's all. They're only probably-here in our own specious present. Their probability of being here oscillates in time, wherever they direct their attention—the same way as the thing you're looking at in your field of vision seems more real, while you focus on it, though the rest's still there. They're like particles with resonance peaks, Commander. They could be anywhere—any-time! They're most probable at certain times—though actually they spread over all the possible timespan open to them. And we can feel this. Oh yes, we can feel it. Our reality is dictated by them."

"Ridiculous. A being can't shuttle about in time."

"They don't *shuttle*. They extend over a longer period than we do. What the hell is time, anyway? It's only a way of relating events and measuring them. It doesn't exist on its own."

"That doesn't explain how they could de-ink that water."

"Yes, it damn well does. Tracking backwards, from *our* point of view, they *seem* to influence events towards previous states . . . They're only really amplifying an earlier bit of their own specious present, the way we focus more attention on an object when we look at it; only the world isn't made of objects, Commander, it's made of processes, events. We're only observers spread out in space, but they can be *unobservers* too—unobserving events happening, as they track back. Like the ink in the water. They didn't de-ink it. I inked it, actually, when we saw your little ship coming down. As a demonstration. They unobserved it for your benefit, to show you. I knew they would. We're luckier than frogs. At least we can share in their world a little. We see their unobservations. We see the ripples converging on the pebble thrown in the pond. We see the world fluctuating backwards and forwards. Children weren't born to us after a while . . . because the moment of conception becomes the *separating* of the sperm from the egg!"

"More likely because they had the urge drained out of them," I whispered to Commander Marinetti.

"They don't hate us; they drew us here, to the center, to care for us, Commander! Oh, it started about the second year, I guess. Dreams first. Our dreams running backwards . . . Have you ever dreamt backwards, Commander? It's much easier for them to influence a dream . . . Dreaming backwards was just our preparation for the same thing happening in waking life. It was the habituation of our minds to sense what they sense."

"The ink thing happened," Resnick protested. "Look, I saw it happen. It did violate thermodynamics!"

"No, it was just one *way* of seeing what happened, inside the span of a present that included the whole event. The world stays conserved for them. They know much more about the workings of our minds now. They've studied us."

"So they see things differently from us. Or so you say. How did this stop your animals breeding?" demanded Marinetti, taking my point about the possible psychological block in the colonists' case.

"Ah," grinned Greenberg slyly, "there was no way of conceiving the world. So there was no way of conceiving in it, either."

"Those are just words, man."

Greenberg cackled inanely. "Do you think we have the language for discussing this, Commander? We're like the frog's eye and brain, built to notice something utterly limited. Why do you suppose the word 'conceive' ties Thought and Life together so neatly?"

"A frog still lays eggs that hatch successfully, whatever we think of the universe, Mr. Greenberg."

"Alas, if only we were frogs then . . . We had some luck with the chickens for a time. Even they were a shade too bright. Capable of being influenced . . . Or maybe we didn't look after them properly, we had other things on our minds by then."

That was more likely, I thought! The Fairies had very effectively sabotaged our settlers—by getting them to do it themselves!

Marinetti looked close to tears; but he was drying them before an inner fire of angry duty.

"I expect you want to be evacuated, now?"

"Back to Earth? To insane hospitals? Oh no, this is our world. We live here. We're learning to know it. Know them. I realize that there won't be any kids to carry on the work . . ."

"What work?" sneered Marinetti.

"The work of learning, of course."

"Learning what? To survive here?"

"No, you idiot, the work of finding out what this world is. That's all. We live here, don't you see? We've been learning to understand too long to give up now. Anyway, I'm sure they like us. Or the crops wouldn't thrive—"

"You're abject."

"A man has one life, then it ends. We have our lives to lead, and finish them. Then the whole event will have taken place. We will have seen it out. Don't you realize," Greenberg whispered urgently, "we will have known the whole lifespan of Man on this world, when the last one of us dies? The whole experience will have been acted out by us personally. We will have shown them an event lasting fifty or sixty years and, what's more, that we are satisfied with this event! This will be our full true span of knowledge—longer, far longer, than theirs! We'll win, in dying."

"It's dreadful," murmured Marinetti. "We can't take them back to Earth. They're aliens now. How can we leave them here, though, like this?"

"You can leave us," shouted Greenberg, overhearing, "because we damn well are aliens. What did you expect, dumping us here? That you'd find a world peopled with human beings? Now, Mister Commander, Sir, I have other things to think about. More important things. You caused a lot of upset, landing here again. You had no right to."

And off he stalked. And the other colonists too, leaving us alone to find our own way back to the survey craft.

"We can't evacuate them. Definitely," Marinetti told us as we walked out through the contemptible mini-suburb. "We can't take this absurd defeat back to Earth from the stars."

"On the other hand," said Laura Philipson, "if any of it's true, aren't the aliens here terribly important? What are they? *How* are they? What do they mean? They could change our whole concept structure. I feel . . . this may be the major discovery of the whole journey. And the colonists are our only tool for knowing. Oughtn't we try to take them back for that reason, whatever they wish? This mightn't seem such a failure, then. This might seem one of the great breakthroughs in our knowledge."

I myself nodded, half convinced. Because, frustrating, depressing, and damping of all our hopes for a viable colony though this was, at least (and at last) something out of the ordinary had happened. Almost, I thought bizarrely, worth losing one world—to gain a whole unexpected dimension.

"We've no way to force them, even if we wanted to," Resnick retorted. "Besides, I think it's downright dangerous to stay here a moment longer than we have to. We all saw that blob of ink return to its starting point, from inky water. We saw it. Us. The new arrivals. We can be influenced in a way we never were during all those months building the colony originally. We've left our human 'specimens' here. The Fairies have found out about us. If Greenberg's telling the truth, they've put us through a rats' maze, with walls made of time instead of space. It needs a separate special scientific expedition, taking precautions we can't take."

"The last colonist will be dead by the time that

could get here," argued Laura. "Forty years' experience wasted . . . what to do then? Plant another colony of people and let them be affected like laboratory animals? Hardly!"

Marinetti looked frustrated, dried up; dehydrated of his hopes. But he refused to stay. "The main thing is to take the facts back to Earth, not the casualties," he told us flatly, drably.

"It isn't so bad," I reassured. "There's the whole future. There'll be star travel, communication. This is only the first starship. The problem of Haven can wait another hundred years, or a thousand years—if it has to. We'll be back. Some human beings will, that is. They'll know what to expect."

So Laura flew our little ship back up to *Starseeder* and we made ready to light the fusion torch.

Fairies—or a fairy—on board *Starseeder*. Can't catch them, can't even film them to prove it. Now you see them, now you don't. Even this isn't true, since they aren't completely present, riding their wave of probability back and forth, dodging us, keeping their amplitude peaks out of phase with our brief specious present. All the time they're living slightly in the past or future. They just ghost *via* us briefly, momentarily, yet not present enough to catch. Maybe there's only one that slipped on board the survey craft. How to tell?

One is enough. Astrophysics reports ridiculous observations: quasars blue-shifting towards us, as though the universe is contracting in on itself with us at the center of focus. It can't be the case, or the whole sky would be blazing with inpouring radiation. And yet . . . perhaps it is . . . for microseconds? Some sensors overload and burn out. Still, the quasar and far galaxy observations aren't constant—they fluctuate. We have to joke that a fairy is in the equipment, and disregard them.

One of the technicians puts a bowl of milk and a saucer of food scraps outside his cabin door. He says he was figuring on a new improved fairytrap. No sign of the trap, though, only the bowl and the saucer. Marinetti reprimands him for stupidity. But in a kindly way.

Swanson, Navigator-Astronomer, is blinded in one eye by a flaring up of light when he looks through the optical scope for a star-fix. His skin is deeply sunburnt around the eye. The retina is destroyed, burnt out. By all the light in the universe, pouring inwards.

It cannot be that way.

We've set our course, now, not by star-fix, but by computer course memory and radio-maps. Too risky to look outside directly. Automating the opticals only results in equipment overloading, even before dampers intervene. If we didn't know that the outside termperature of space is still steady a shade above absolute zero, we might be forgiven for assuming that the universe was indeed imploding in a storm of light and radiation, from time to time, at random. As it is, we have to accept that somehow we perceive the expansion of the universe in reverse, for brief moments. Do our instruments really perceive this too? Or do we only perceive them as doing it—while that Fairy is "unobserving" us? How was Swanson's eye burnt? Do we only hallucinate that it is burnt?

Critical surges in the fusion drive, as it accelerates us to translight transition. Impossible to hold the magnetic plasma steady when currents are liable to alternate and fluctuate like this at random. We switch the drive off, having only achieved one thousandth of light-speed, nowhere near to transition point. Now we're drifting, hopefully in the direction of Sol; though Sol will have moved out of our path by the time we arrive there, approximately 8,000 years from now at our present velocity. So we blend arsenic compounds in the lab and put out other saucers and dishes of food and milk, doped with the poison. They are accepted. Joy! The dishes are licked clean. Thank God for that.

There's a pool of arsenic-laced milk and a heap of arsenic-laced food, undigested, on the floor in the same position where the bowl and saucer were yesterday. The bait has been uneaten; undrunken. Can I say that, since it was originally drunk and eaten? It had been de-eaten, de-drunk; earlier in the same moment of fairy time as it was consumed in, later on in our own time.

On we drift, 8,000 years away from Earth. Now, that really is a time-span to conjure with! I'm thinking a lot about the time-spans now. Last night, for the first time, I dreamed a dream backwards.

Backwards dream a dreamed I.

ON COOKING THE FIRST HERO IN SPRING

When we finally landed, through miles of hazy cloud, the Clayfolk (as we decided to call them) seemed oblivious of the silver ship settling in their midst and went about their business, plastering walls, molding pots, and gathering food. They looked like upright, bifurcate slugs, with bodies that stretched and contracted as they walked, producing a curious undulating pogostick effect. They could pop out any number of pseudopod fingers at will from the ends of their arms, like clusters of snails' horns, then resorb them back into the wrist stumps. Proof of their culture lay all around us: the huts, the pottery, the cooking fires. Yet their blank indifference bothered us. Was this really intelligent behavior?

As soon as we left the ship, however, the sight of three aliens in sealed suits galvanized them. They flowed about us, prodded us, patted up, and Rhoda was able to record her first samples of the Clayfolk speech as they made noises at us and about us.

Rhoda was a lithe young Negress, Lobsang a middle-aged Tibetan male, and I, as you can see, am a red-haired Celt, as speckled with freckles as any hen. Our features showed through our face plates, but the basic impression our suits gave was one of perfect triplet identity. It was this fact that disturbed the Clayfolk. But we only cottoned on to that later . . . (If indeed that *was* the truth.)

Now even I, a mere pilot, and no linguist or social scientist, very soon realized that if the noises they were making were speech, it was a very queer form of it. All the time, that same slobbery glutinous bark; it never varied! After five minutes of it, Rhoda switched her squawk box off in disgust. A language composed of one single word? Preposterous.

Yet as we wandered round their village, it was impossible to avoid the impression of civilization. Cones and cupola clay huts formed a perfect double circle around a central plaza dominated by a large hearth with a roasting spit. The one break in this circle led out along a straight avenue lined by rows of circular clay statues (seemingly of Clayfolk bending over to touch their toes) disappearing into the mists. And the cooking spit itself—made from stalactites bound together by strong fibers! I was amazed at how they'd managed to fashion such a piece of equipment on this soft, wet world, in the absence of metals or firm wood or even, apparently, of hard bones. No charred ribs or femurs lay near the hearth, and their own floppy, rubbery bodies seemed to have nothing stiffer than gristle in them. There was, too, their miraculous mastery of fire, on a world visibly bereft of flints or striking stones, without two dry sticks to rub together.

"If I hear that word once more!" growled Rhoda, as the Clayfolk gestured at their spit, their pots, the roots and fungi and giant snails cooking in them, and named them all urgently for us, all with the same name . . .

"One word contains all words," remarked Lobsang mystically. "All words dissolve into one."

Naturally he was happy that we were going to have to rely on his trance technique for a cultural pattern, rather than on Rhoda's squawk box; that is, her GCSU (General Culture Structures Unit)—which doesn't translate anything as such, but sets up algebraic maps based on whatever communication system inhabitants use, whether sounds, or light patterns as with the Giant Squids of the Sigma Draconis ocean-world, or gestures as with the Mutes of the thunderous Aldebaran planet.

"What's that mean?" she grumbled.

"Well, if you repeat the same word over and over enough times, you start hearing different words, don't you? Maybe these folk actually hear a whole set of different words? But there's consensus on the meanings, because they're linked in some way, empathy, telepathy? It's an idea."

"A very foggy one!"

"Foggy place," retorted Lob.

"Their gestures," I suggested diplomatically. "Like Aldebaran, maybe? They're continually pointing and fingering."

Rhoda shook her head dismissively.

"They point at the same object with any number of fingers—or none at all. I've been watching, it's all random."

"Then I shall prepare my mind for the trance," Lob concluded gleefully. "My privilege, when

your methods fail. In my contract, no? We don't
have long here. These beings shall become phantasms and projections of my own mind. I shall
become mad and incorporate them."

Rhoda had little time to feel chagrined, though,
for it was just then that the landscape began to
change around us . . .

Well, we weren't exactly taken by surprise! In
orbit, we'd spent long enough surveying the re-
spective motions of star, gasgiant, and moon, to
forsee some pretty weird days for the latter so far
as "daylight" went.

The gasgiant itself, a dazzling blue, had only
failed by a few per cent mass to become a second
partner star to the bright orange primary. The
giant moon was perched precariously just a few
thousand miles beyond the Roche limit, that
should have broken it into a billion pieces and
spread it out like Saturn's rings had it been any
closer. Yet it was unbraked by tidal forces. Every
hundred years or so the furthest planet of this
system rushed in on a cometary ellipse that took it
inside the gasgiant's orbit and out again—
whipping the moon like a top, just enough to
compensate for the braking effect.

We foresaw phases of orange sunlight, phases
of blue planetlight, phases of bright purple com-
binedlight, and finally nights black as pitch
whenever the moon faced neither luminary.
Phases could be prolonged, annulled, repeated,
however, in a quasi-random tic-tac-toe fashion,
on account of the way the moon both spun, and
tumbled, at once. An overall pattern only really

emerged in terms of decades according to our computer's calculations. That life had arisen, and persisted, on such a world seemed fairly remarkable; that it was apparently intelligent frankly astonished us. Yet slave-drones had sent back TV footage of the Clayfolk village (easily spottable on infra-red from the heat of the fires). We had to accept their existence, illogical as it was! Naturally, they couldn't have any real understanding of the true circumstances of their world, astronomically, buried away beneath that persistent cloud veil. Things must seem highly mutable to them. "Seasons" and "years" would be meaningless terms. Even "days" must be highly flexible and unpredictable. Rhoda expected a novel and interesting language to emerge to cope with this confusion (but never, poor lady, a language of one word!).

So, as I say, the landscape shifted.

From the blue planetlight phase, to the bright purple of sun and gasgiant in the sky together; and if you think of purple as a dark color, think again. It positively *ached* at us, till we had to lower the shades in our helmets.

This light change wrought new shapes and contours in the landscape, and erased the old. The blurred shadows we cast now were twin ones; yet each separate shadow seemed to *project* a cone of light instead of deleting light. Red and blue splotches accompanied us that seemed somehow more genuine than the prevalent violent purple.

Vegetation underwent a rapid change. Fungi wilted and dissolved. Ferns we hadn't seen before unfurled, fast as a time-lapse movie. Dragonflies hatched and took wing. Worms writhed out of the mud and leapt to catch them in tiny piranha mouths.

The Clayfolk speeded up too, to scoop these worms into pots, all the while chattering animatedly our by now least favorite word.

"My God," groaned Rhoda, "it might as well be a different world now, just look at it! And still they go on saying "that's", "That's, "that's" to it." She mimicked the Clayfolk "word" venomously, giving it an interpretation that it may (or may not) have had.

"In sameness, is difference," chuckled Lob-sang.

The Clayfolk took no more interest in us right now. We might as well have been invisible; though none of them actually collided with us, I noticed.

"Enough for one day," Rhoda said decisively. "Let's look round the village separately, then get some sleep. Try your luck tomorrow, Lob."

" 'Day'?" chuckled Lob later, as we made our way back to the ship, together, through worms and ferns and dragonflies, accompanied by our brighter, more real double shadows, "or 'season'? Tomorrow, or next year?"

To which, of course, Rhoda had no answer; since it was either, or neither, or both.

When we woke up eight hours later (by ship time) it was pitchblack night, and it stayed that way for two of our days. While we waited for a new dawn, we discussed that avenue of statues—and realized that none of us had actually stepped outside the

village to take a closer look at any of them. It was
as though the shape of the village was somehow
self-sufficient, had penned us in without our
knowing it! We spoke of possible kinship patterns
for the Clayfolk—another way of getting inside
their minds—and discovered that none of us had
unearthed the least evidence of how they bred
even. Live births, laying of eggs, fission? Why
hadn't we thought to ask ourselves why we
hadn't, till now? Maybe the constant undulations
of their bodies had hopelessly blurred age and sex
distinctions to such an extent that we actually
found it difficult to think about them until we
were back in our neat, functional, logical ship
again, with our suits off and our own differences
consequently obvious.

"Maybe they melt in the dark to reform next
daylight," offered Lob ironically.

"Ah, the dark!" snapped Rhoda. "Now, there's
one thing they must have a name for, different
from the light!"

"What point is there in naming the dark, when
you can't see anything in it?"

"What I mean, you obtuse Sherpa, is there'll
always be a spring or morning time that's quite
distinct! I'm damned if I see how they ever
civilized themselves, with all the other confu-
sions. Yet how did they develop a concept of
regularity—as witness that line of statues? The
key must lie in the dawn!"

She was right. It did indeed. But hardly in the
way she expected!

Shortly after we'd slept again and awoken to eat

another breakfast in the dark, it dawned—a bright ruddy orange dawn, from the Sun-alone. We watched from the cabin window as the Clayfolk swarmed out of their huts towards that spit at the heart of the village; and, in horror, the use they actually put that piece of equipment to . . .

They seized one of their own number out of the crowd, slung him over the cooking spit and wrapped him round it flexibly, binding his feet and head together. One Clayman stuck long, thin clay pipes into the victims' mouth, nostrils and rectum. Another kindled a fire beneath the spit. A third began cranking the handle to turn it. Others slapped wet clay onto the victim's body.

"Those figures outside the village, along the road! They're not statues at all," cried Rhoda. "They're them, *themselves!*"

"They must breed rather rapidly," observed Lobsang with equanimity. He was already gearing his mind to regard all Clayfolk as equivalent to phantasms from the *Tibetan Book of the Dead*— purely subjective demons of the mind, that couldn't ever trap the man who realized this. "Quite an attrition rate for a little village to bear . . . if they sacrifice to the dawn every day like this!"

"Sacrifice? Oh, they are doing something, certainly, the demons. But who knows what?"

"What are those pipes for?" she whimpered. "In his face and his behind."

"Stop him exploding as they heat him up," I said, ever the practical engineer. "Let the hot air out." Managing to sound tough, but equally appalled, to tell the truth.

The fire glowed, they turned the spit, slapping on fresh clay as the first coat hardened.

And we watched what had once been a living alien being transformed slowly and methodically into something far more alien and hideous—something which we, in our rashness, had glibly classified among "works of art" not so long ago. At what stage in the cooking process the poor tortured being inside that clay case ceased to be alive, I do not know. I only hoped it was soon, but I feared not, given the elaborate precautions to prevent early asphyxiation; as I now saw those pipes also to be. At least we were spared, by the ship's solid hull, from hearing the being's screams.

The cooking went on for half an hour, till the circular statue was completed to their satisfaction; then they doused the fire, and let the thing cool.

When it had cooled enough, a triumphal procession of the Clayfolk hauled it away on a stalactite pole, down along the Road of Statues.

"I suppose we have a history of human sacrifices ourselves," muttered Rhoda. "People being cooked in bronze bulls and burnt at stakes . . . I guess if dawn is the only fixed point in their world it's only predictable they'd worship it pretty fiercely."

"Worship? You do leap to conclusions, Rhoda."

"Do you have any better explanation? It certainly isn't a fertility rite!"

"I shall apply my fertile imagination to what it is. Lamas may slip in, where squawk boxes fear to tred, eh?"

Which was perfectly true. As the human race rapidly found out in its explorations among the stars, the alien wears many garbs—which socio-mathematical disciplines, the like of Rhoda's, couldn't necessarily always penetrate. Usually she did well enough—and Lob found his time taken up tidying phonemes and smoothing out kinks in her algebras of alien world views (being a trained ethnomathematician, as well as a lamaist magician)—and only occasionally asked Lob to help out with a trance insight when she ran up against some hopelessly alien cultural pattern. But this time she had run into a stone wall right at the very start, with a vengeance: a stone wall with precisely one stone in it!

Lobsang was an adept in the Tibetan chöd ritual, where the celebrant offers himself up body and soul as a banquet for alien demons and imagines himself devoured by them, and a proficient in the various maps of hell-worlds and paradise-worlds of the Bardo Thödol, the Book of the Dead. So very remote from earthly reality, Lobsang could shortcut his way, via such psychic netherlands, into alien mindscapes that resisted Rhoda's science; seeing all forms of being, from his Tibetan heights, as mere fluxes in the same universal illusion. If there was a wall here, then he would burrow under it: fearlessly, with peace of mind. The Tibetan chöd banquet was a more gruelling, gruesome business than this cooking of the Clayman, the way Lob had described it! The sense of one's bowels being torn out, one's veins sucked dry, the marrow spooned from one's bones by demons! To experience all this—and believe it to be literally happening—yet observe it all with perfect composure . . . Lob was well prepared psychologically.

So, when the Clayfolk flocked back to the village to resume their peaceful, softly-flowing tasks, Lob went out there with us, right to the patch of ground before the hearth, and drew a white mandala outline on the mud with an aerosol spraycan—he called the shape a *kyilkhor* in his native Tibetan. Entering his magic diagram, he squatted down cross-legged.

The Clayfolk flowed around the lines of the *kyilkhor*, touching gently, murmuring that word of theirs. Lob began chanting to himself in Tibetan, a monotonous sing-song refrain to lull himself into a trance:

"Zab-chö shi-hto gong-pa rang-döl lay bar-doi thö-dol chen-mo chö-nyid bar-doi ngo-töd zhu-so . . ." he sang, with superb breath control, his eyes staring wide behind his faceplate, not seeing us at all though we knew he would return briefly, between wave peaks of the trance, to report the situation as he saw it . . .

"The shapes flow, the colors change, the world walks backwards," sang Lob after a while in English, staring at us sightlessly.

"Yet we are thinking beings. We make, we build. Yet this world flows to and fro in madness. All we can say is that a thing *is*, for the time that it is. Not *what* it is, since it may not be again. A hand, a shadow, a color. We must put a thing into itself and see how it fits. Then *it is*, and *other things* are. The fitting of a thing into its own shape is the shape of our agreement. The putting of oneself into oneself is the Making, at the dawn . . ."

"That's why the Clayman is tortured?"

"We feel astonished by our agreement," Lob chanted on. "The sheer possibility of agreement on anything. But should we give thanks to the lights in the sky that we are in agreement? Shall we make gods? Is that what this is, this putting of oneself into oneself? No, it is the prevention of a god! One is a hero, who fits into oneself. If one did not fit into oneself, every dawn, there would be no rules. If one says something different every day, is that *a* rule? Pain stops the world, in a cry. The cry is the picture of pain. Thus the pain pictures the world . . ."

Then Lob was swimming through alien waves again, seeing us, he later told us, from their viewpoint. What delighted them most was our inflexible similarity. We were three heroes, baked into our suits. Our ship, a single random object, meant nothing compared to our three suited selves. Yet as soon as we uttered noises, we outraged them. However fervently they corrected us we failed to make the same sounds twice running. As heroes, we affirmed the being of the world; yet denied it by our every word, so that, in effect, we cancelled ourselves right out for them. We no longer had existence, in their eyes. So they ignored us.

Of course, this was only Lob's *Bardo*-vision version—his own effort to fit things into themselves so that they made sense! We could feel free to take it with a pinch of salt.

"Chen-mo chö-nyid bar-doi ngo-töd zhu-so," chanted Lob; then with a great bound he skipped out of the magic circle and hustled us back to the ship urgently, to tell us more of the way he saw the Clayfolk as seeing things, before the intuitions slipped from his grasp.

We stood by the window, watching Clayfolk molding clay with variable numbers of extruded fingers, their bodies bobbing and undulating in the orange mists. While we watched, the gasgiant planet rose to join the sun in the sky, and there were double shadows in the village again that appeared to cast light, not mask it: then not long afterwards the gasgiant set again below the same westward horizon, casting the day backwards towards morning.

"Don't we torture the world into categories, in our own way?" grinned Lob lopsidedly. "With words and symbols—English, Tibetan, Syrian . . . They must be the noblest logicians in the universe, these. Number can hardly exist for them, yet they affirm series. Cause constantly cancels logic out because they can't see into outer space to know the true causes of these strange effects. Yet they affirm logic. They deny the very evidence of their senses for the sake of it. Only thus is culture possible for them. Only thus can there be rules from day to day, and any form of time-binding. Yet they can't *speak* about their world, because to do so destroys logic."

"An intelligent species must use language of some sort to be classified intelligent! What are these, then? Automata? Is this just an illusion of culture out there? The pots. The huts. You say they're logical beings."

"Ah, but strictly they aren't so much *logical* beings, as logic personified, Rhoda. They're propositions, essences. They can't afford language here, it's too destructive."

"Then they're not intelligent compared with us."

"We seem like nothing to them, Rhoda. They are reality perpetually reasserting itself in the midst of the ocean of becoming."

"They're zombies. And ghouls. You've let your imagination run riot this time, Lob."

"Certainly it's in my imagination. It's because I have internalized them in my trance, that's why it's true. They have group sensitivity, you see. Empathy. They share their hero's pain. Pain's the only concept we really *have* to communicate urgently, to stop it, don't you see? Only in this way can a name arise, of necessity, with its own internal truth. Then they can safely apply its truth to everything.

"But they can't name this world any other way, except by fitting themselves into their own shape; the world into its own shape, by extension. Really, it's the same with the universe at large. Only we never dare acknowledge it. What is a universe? I ask myself. One thing, by definition. The totality of all there is. There's nothing to compare it with. All you can do is put the thing into itself and see what it fits. They've got the right idea. We must attend the next dawn cooking, to hear it for ourselves."

"Too tricky," warned Rhoda. "They may want to bake us this time."

Lob shook his head.

"We're quite safe, we're invisible now. Only Clayfolk make heroes. Only they can fit into themselves. We failed."

So, despite Rhoda's qualms, we were present at the village hearth during the next dawning when the Clayfolk swarmed to greet the light; in this instance, light from a simultaneous rising of the sun in the north-west, and gasgiant in the south-east. Amid purple mists and binary shadows we invisibles watched the spit put to use again; a Clayman folded over it, the fire kindled, the clay slapped on by many fingers, the pipes stuck in his mouth and nostrils and his rectum. I held Rhoda's hand, to comfort her.

That cry of pain came again and again through the clay pipes stuck in the being's mouth, as he turned, and baked, inside the clay suit: and we heard that selfsame glottal slobbery bark as had assaulted our ears since we first set foot on the Clayworld.

"I name this reality, Pain," sang Lob. "We stand at the place where the only real word is given utterance. It is the compact of agreement. It affirms What-Is."

Then, in a more conversational tone, jerking his thumb at the avenue of bent-over statues, he added: "That isn't really a road at all. Essentially it doesn't lead anywhere; it just leads."

"A road must go some place!"

"Why, Rhoda? That isn't a highway, it's a rule, a series. And its statues aren't statues, they're definitions. Each is a fitting-into-itself. But I don't advise we pursue the Clayfolk out along it, we mightn't find our way back so easily . . ."

After a time the cry died away into a sigh that might have been simply the natural passage of air through that thing on the spit. However the Clayfolk had already taken the word up, and were repeating it over and over, gesturing at everything in their world.

"Admit it, Lob, it's a nonsense interpretation," insisted Rhoda while I piloted us up through the clouds towards the clarity of space. She addressed Lob harshly and petulantly, as though he was guilty of a crime. He only bowed his head and meditated.

Then a solar system was around us once again, obeying sensible laws; and stars in their constellations and clusters; and the far smudges of galaxies. Ahead lay the mother ship; silver dragonfly with bulbous head where we had our living quarters, long slim tail terminating in the knob of the plasma drive, and wings spread to harvest the interstellar hydrogen magnetically. We all sighed with relief, even Lob.

Later, we classified the aberrant moon as UIS—Uninhabited by an Intelligent Species; dominant native life-form a biped slug with a high degree of constructive activity, instinctively programmed. By general consent Lobsang's version was vetoed. I think even Lob was happy to be overruled this time. We sped away to more substantial worlds, where his insights served us well enough, subsequently.

I haven't time to tell about his breakthrough with the fire beings of Achernar IV or the slime molds of Deneb VII. But it must have been an off-day for him, that time on the Clayworld. Yet he never quite admitted it. He had his pride—as Rhoda had hers. After all, a Sherpa had been joint-first on the summit of Everest on Earth. And the universe was our Everest now—an Everest without apparent summit.

THE EVENT HORIZON

For the second time in three years the starship *Subrahmanyan Chandrasekhar* sailed for the Black Hole that was the blind eye of the binary system Epsilon Aurigae, with the Arab tele-medium Habib on board.

At about the same distance from the bright supergiant that is the visible partner of the system as Pluto from the Sun, they reached their destination. Officers and scientists crowded the nacelle beside the lounge to stare into space at something they couldn't see except insofar as it bent light from the background stars around itself in an annulus of secondary ghost images.

The Hole itself was nothing—literally. Even the fabric of space was missing, there.

A nova is fearful; a supernova, awe-inspiring. Yet their ravening energies are a creative mainspring of the galaxy, spewing out heavy elements for new stars and planets. They are positive energies. The mind can grasp them. But the Black Hole is all negative—the emptiness of the void multiplied a million times into something infinitely greedy. A star collapses under its own gravity, disappears from the universe and leaves a whirlpool of nothingness beyond it. Anything falling into the hole—no matter how well pro-

tected it is, no matter if it is powered by the energy
of a thousand suns—is trapped forever. The Black
Hole is Death the Conqueror.

The Hole in the Aurigae system had already
been located from Earth in the twentieth century
by its periodic eclipses of its yellow supergiant
partner every twenty-seven years; however it
wasn't till the mid-twenty-third that a starship
brushed by it.

Then, something more incredible than the Hole
itself was found—a living being trapped inside it.

The growth of Psionics Communications—the
telemedium system—made the discovery possible. Instantaneous psi-force alone could enter a
Black Hole and emerge again. But only if a mind
was already present in there . . .

In the nacelle, along with the officers and scientists, were the two political officers from Bu-
Psych-Sec—the Bureau of Psychological Security—Lew Boyd and Liz Nielstrom; Habib,
who had first made contact with the mind in
there; and a young Swedish girl on her first
starflight, Mara Glas.

Habib stood out from the others by wearing
traditional Arab costume: the *haik* and *aba* of the
desert Bedouin. He wore the headdress and long
full skirt with a striped white and blue mantle of
camel-hair sacking pulled over it. By making a
clown of himself in this way, parodying his un-
educated nomad's origin, he made himself ac-
ceptable to the others and guarded the privacy of
his feelings; another strategy was his carefully
cultivated gutter humor. He was that freak thing, a

mind-whore; and however essential he might be for communications and psychological stability, the telemedium was a reluctant actor in a perpetual dirty joke.

Psionics and sexual energy were the two great forces that Bu-Psych-Sec had learned to harness to bind starships safely to home-base Earth no matter how far they roamed. Through psi and sex, bonded together, Earth held her star fleet on the tightest leash, a leash rooted so deeply in the nervous system as to guarantee there would never be any defections to lotus worlds among the stars; nor more mundane lapses in her continual on-line monitoring of the farthest vessel.

As they stood in the nacelle, Mara Glas tried telling herself for the hundredth time that this was all for the good of everyone at home on Earth, and for the stability of civilization; that Bu-Psych-Sec had designed the safest, most humanitarian system compatible with star empire. So she had been programmed to believe at any rate, by days of lectures and subliminal persuasion.

But she never thought it would be like this, serving Earth's starship communications system. She never dreamed.

Naturally, the Black Hole was fair pretext for a bout of boisterous smut, if only to mask their fear of the phenomenon. The very name carried such blatant connotations of the trance room that Mara thanked her stars she wasn't born a Negress; felt pity for Habib's darker-skinned soul.

"There she blows!" crowed the chief engineer.

Ted Ohashi, the astrophysicist from Hawaii—a

mess of a man, like a third-rate Sumo wrestler gone to seed—snickered back:

"That little mouth; she'll suck all the juice in the galaxy given half a chance."

"A suck job, that's good, I like it," laughed Kurt Spiegel, the leonine Prussian from Hamburg's Institut für Physik, boisterously. His wiry hair was swept back in a mane as though the abstractions of Physics had electrified it; though just as exciting to the man, in fact, was that other district of Hamburg around the Repperbahn, St. Pauli, where he got his relief from the enigmas of Schwarzschildian Geometry and Pauli Equations in the more down-to-earth contortions of the strippers going through their bump and grind routines for him, drunk on Schnapps, replete on bockwurst.

Habib made a point of joining in the merriment, while Liz Nielstrom flashed a grin of pure malice at Mara for failing to join in.

How the human race struggled against Beauty! Mara wept silently. How desperately they strove to make the Singular and Remarkable, dirty and shameful!

Mara was young. With the perpetual rush to draft telemediums into the Navy, and the fewness of those with the potential among Earth's billions, the Swedish girl was barely out of her fifteenth year before being drafted.

One thing she didn't know about Habib was the kind of debriefing Bu-Psych-Sec put him through after the first expedition, when he reported the existence of that mind inside the Black Hole to the incredulity of practically everyone in the Navy. They'd peeled his mind down like an onion at the Navy Hospital in Annapolis. They'd used strobehypno on him. Neoscopalamine. Pentathol-plus. Deepsee. It had been a harrowing, insane-making three weeks before they believed him. And it was another two years before the second expedition sailed.

But one thing she did know about him, that no one else did, was the utter difference between the image he presented publicly of a dirty street Arab, and the sense of his mind she had whenever they'd taken the psionic trigger drug, 2-4 Psilo-C, together, to cathect with Earth across the void. Then it was like a light being switched on in a dark room, and he was a different Habib—a Bedouin of the sands, a poet, and a prophet.

The people who rode the carrier beam of the teletrance never knew the pure beauty of the desert between the stars. All they got a sense of was the dirty urchin hanging around the oasis of far Earth, plucking at their sleeves and mumbling, "Mister, you want to buy my sister?" But Habib was the desert Bedouin too. Why did he always deny the desert beauty, out of trance?

Maybe this was the last lesson she had to learn—the final breaking in of the foal, to insure she could be safely graduated with flying colors and posted to some star frigate by herself.

Just then, strangely, as though he was reading her thoughts out of trance, Habib grasped her arm softly and whispered in her ear, with the voice that she'd longed to hear from his lips for the past three months—yet quietly, so that no one else could hear:

"Compared with the void of space, Mara, whatever is the void inside that thing?"

He asked her gently and eerily—as though the

Mecca pilgrimage of their minds was at last underway and the furtive shabbiness of the caravanserais, the whores and beggary and disease, could be put behind them.

"It is so *solid* a void that 'here' and 'there' are meaningless words. There will be no referents in there, except those you yourself manufacture, Mara . . ."

But could she really trust this sudden shift from urchin to muezzin calling the faithful to prayer—or was it just another round in the game of cruelty?

"It's so dense in there that it must be like swimming through stone." Habib went on murmuring in her ear. "Yet even that comparison's no good, for *he* has no power to swim about his dwelling place—"

Puzzled, Mara stared out without replying.

The captain stepped into the nacelle a moment later—a thick-set, hard-headed grandson of Polish-German immigrants to America, who still had the air of being a peasant in from the country dressed in his best, ill-tailored suit, and who ran the ship with all the cunning and blunt persistence of the peasant making a profitable pig sale: this, alloyed to a degree or two in Astronavigation and a star or two for combat in some brushfire war in Central Africa stirred up by the draft board's "child-snatching." Immune to the wonders of space, Lodwy Rinehart barely glanced outside.

"May I have your attention a moment? We'll be sailing down to the ergosphere commencing twenty hundred hours—"

Ted Ohashi gobbled nervously:

"You mean tonight? Maybe we should fire a few drones near that thing first, to check the stability of the ergosphere—"

"After three months you want to hang back another few days? Maybe you want another session with Mara Glas in case you get killed and never know those joys again, is that it? Sorry, Dr. Ohashi. Twenty hundred, we're going right down on her up to the hilt."

"Just not too close," the fat man pleaded. "We could be sucked in, you know. Space is so bent there. No power could get us out then. Fifty nautical miles off the top of the ergosphere's fine by me, Captain!"

"Point taken, Dr. Ohashi," Rinehart smiled acidly. "That's also fine by me. 'Up to the hilt' was just a colorful bit of naval slang. Need I spell it out for you?"

The German from Hamburg guffawed. "That's good, I like it, Captain."

The Hawaiian snickered dutifully too then, his fat wobbling in the starlight, but he was scared.

Mara shivered. Habib shrugged indifferently; by shrugging he hid his features in the shadow of the haik . . .

Space presents itself to the telemedium's mind in symbolic form. The mind can only see what it has learned to see, and it has certainly not learned to see light-years and cosmic rays and gravity waves. Therefore space must present itself in terms of symbols learned by the brain during the cognitive processes of life on Earth.

The symbols Habib presented Mara with were

those of the desert Bedouin. Perhaps, taught by
someone from her own part of the world, she
would have learned to see the wastelands of the
arctic tundra, the icefloes of the northern seas, or
endless flows of forest. But Habib presented her
with the golden desert—and for this she thanked
him from the bottom of her heart, for its pure
beauty had a wealth of heat and color—stark as it
was—that awakened her Swedish soul to life, as
the brief hot summer awakened her country from
its wintry melancholy once a year.

She remembered so clearly the surprise of that
first cathexis with Earth across the light-years, in
company with Habib . . .

Every Navy man had the right and duty to
cathect with Earth through the ship's telemedium. At the other end of the link would be a
home-based telemedium ridden by one of Bu-
Psych-Sec's professional "Mermaids": forging
what the Reichian-Tantric adepts of Bu-Psych-
Sec liked to refer to as "libidinal cathexis" with
Someone Back Home, therefore with Mother
Earth herself.

The energies of the libido, bottled-up deliberately by sex depressive drugs until the time of
trance, were unleashed upon the responsive
nervous system of the medium in a copulation
that was both physical and transmental. The
energy that ejaculated thought impulses across
the light-years, through a symbolic landscape of
the medium's own devising, had been called different things at different times in history. In the
twentieth century Wilhelm Reich named it Or-
gone Radiation. The Tantric sexual philosophers

of Old India called it, more picturesquely, the
Snake of Kundalini.

Reich had built crude machines to harness and
condense this sexual energy that he believed
permeated space. The Tantrics used yogic asanas
to twist the body into new, prolonged forms of
intercourse; they used the Om chant to make the
nervous system a hypersensitive sounding board;
and hypnotized themselves with yantra diagrams
to send this energy soaring out of the copulating
body through the roof of the skull toward the
stars—toward some subjective cosmic immensi-
ty, at least.

Bu-Psych-Sec had rationalized and blended
Reichian therapy with the Tantric art of love and
yantra meditation. In its crash course for sensitiz-
ing the potential telemediums, much of this learning was force-fed hypnotically in deep sleeps
from which the medium woke, haunted by erotic
cosmic ghosts, to days of pep talks on such topics
as "The Spaceman's Psychological Problems"
and "The Need for Cultural Unity in an Age of
Translight." Yet there could be no live test runs of
the contact techniques till a novice was on his or
her way, light-months from Earth with a super-
visor medium, able to draw on the repressed sexuality of the crew to reach out to another medium
at Bu-Psych-Sec, Annapolis. And every single
trance-trip had to figure economically in terms of
vital Navy information transmitted. Each crew
member riding a medium was subliminally
primed with data that the mermaid at the other
end received the imprint of, to be retrieved by the
drug Deepsee. The Annapolis data banks were

thus constantly updated; and the data copied to other banks hidden deep in the Rocky Mountains. Earth's Navy was not a string of ships, but an integrated nervous system spread out over thousands of cubic light-years.

Yet the doctrines of Reich and Tantra would have been nothing without the development of the trance drug 2-4-Psilo-C. It was an unforeseen spin-off from Bu-Psych-Sec's routine work on psychedelic gases for military and civil policing.

The two crew members who were going to ride Habib and Mara's bodies for the first liberty of the voyage stood twiddling their thumbs with sheepish sleazy grins on their faces, their anticipation of pleasure somewhat muted by the supercilious, sophisticatedly brutal aura of Lew Boyd and his assistant.

The previous Bu-Psych-Sec officer had been more of a therapist in the Masters and Johnson line, with less of the policeman about him. This man Boyd knew his Reich and Tantra inside out, but he carried the stamp of a trouble-shooter from the moment he joined the ship, along with that enigmatic bitch Liz Nielstrom. What kind of relationship had they had been involved in before? Their degree of mental complicity indicated more than a mere working relationship. Yet they didn't seem to have been lovers in the ordinary sense. Rather, they appeared bound together by the cruel magic of their roles, this ugly woman and this smart cop, in a mutual indifference to sex itself except as an instrument of power. Sternly they reveled in the dialectic of the twin faces of authority, the repressive and permissive, gaining their private accord from the games they could play with this psychosexual coin. For them, the galaxy was a gaming table they could amuse themselves at, with the induced Tantric orgasms of others for chips. Professional croupiers of the cosmic naval brothel they were, dedicated to seeing that the Bureau always won, and hunting endlessly for cheats. (But who could possibly cheat? And how?)

There were two couches with encephalographic commune helmets at one end; these helmets swivelled to accept a prone or supine posture . . .

"You can get stripped, the four of you," Liz Nielstrom told them, glancing at her watch. "Earth's standing by."

One of the sailors shuffled about on his feet.

"Excuse me, ma'am, but who's riding the girl; do I get to ride her? I hear it's her first time out," he pleaded.

"It must be your first time too," Nielstrom responded sarcastically. "Since it makes not the least difference to you whether you're riding male or female."

"It's just the idea of it," the sailor mumbled. "So as I'll know afterwards—"

"Think what you like then, sailor. Believe it's her, not him, for all I care. But your request's out of order, and denied."

It was true that it made no difference . . .

Habib slipped off his haik and aba, and stretched out his slim knotty Bedouin body prone on the couch while Nielstrom was busy injecting the two naked sailors in their upper arms. They soon lolled upright in a stupor, awaiting the "Simple Simon Says" command.

Turning to Mara, she gestured the naked girl to take up a supine position on the other couch, where Boyd maneuvered her head carefully into the commune helmet as he had already done for Habib. He pricked her arm with the injection of 2-4-Psilo-C. While Nielstrom carried out her ointmenting of Mara's shaven sex, the light sensation of the other woman's fingers was already slipping away. In the dark of the helmet Mara concentrated her attention on the meditation pattern of the shri yantra diagram. This was an interweaving of upward-pointing and downward-pointing triangles, unfolding from around a central nub. The downward-pointing triangles were female; the upward, male. The central dot was the stored energy, compact in a bud.

Remotely, she heard Boyd give the command—his words slowed down and booming dully, like a tape played at the wrong speed.

"Simple Simon says, make love to Habib, Mr. Monterola! Simple Simon says, make love to Mara, Mr. Nagorski!"

(But it was Monterola who had wanted her.)

Libidinal cathexis started. Time drew further out for her. Distantly, she felt her central bud opening slowly to the man Nagorski's slow thrust. A clammy smell of sweat and the heavy pressure of a body on top of hers receded utterly from her awareness. The yantra opened up hugely, to reveal a vision of symbolic grace through that sexual eye embedded in its heart.

The vision was a beautiful, wonderful thing; something that preliminary training at Bu-Psych-Sec and all the jokes on shipboard had never hinted at . . .

There was a world of magic and beauty, after all. The dreams she'd dreamed as a girl were realities—but secret, hidden realities.

As the drug increased its effect, and Nagorski thrust into her, her sensitivity spread outward: the starship dissolved, her body dissolved, and her mind became a shining mirror seeking for mental images of reflect out there. She was conscious of the nearby presence of Habib; the sense of him varied between shining light and robed, hooded figure whose robes were like sails, like wings. She began to pick up speed together with him, till they were skimming over dunes and dunes of empty golden desert, hunting for the oasis of Earth.

"Beware of mirages," his mind whispered to hers. "Beware of pools that seek to reflect yourself—pools of illusion that would lock you up in their waters. You have to seek the far-off mirror that bears the imprint of another mind within it, like the hallmark on a piece of silver. That's the telecontact you must seek."

He was no dirty-fingered, runny-nosed urchin now, he was the desert hunter, the bird that flies to Mecca, the prophet in the wilderness.

It wasn't so far to Earth, that first cathexis: a half light-year or so. Oasis Earth was still nearby.

The flow of her sensitivity streamed above the empty, thirsty dunes, clutching at Habib's hem. Soon she was flowing into the crowded Oasis where so many streams mixed together, aiming at the tent where Habib beckoned her. Habib held the tent-flap aside for her and they skimmed inside.

The telecontact was a clear pool within the tent; a mirror with the hazy image of the shri yantra floating in it. The two mirrors came together, becoming screens for other minds to use.

The yantra image dissolved: it was no more than a call-sign. There was a time of calm and silence and clarity.

The telemedium was the mirror itself, not the image in the mirror; was the white wall, on which puppet shadows briefly danced and postured and copulated; was the vase of wine for others to get drunk at—but the vase itself doesn't get drunk; was the drum-skin—but not the sticky fingers tapping a rhythm out on to it to set the player's nerves on fire . . .

Mara found herself whispering words to Habib: one slave whispering to another. The words she whispered were poetry.

> There stood upon auction blocks
> In the market of Isfahān
> A thousand and one bodies
> A thousand and one souls . . .
> The souls were like women
> The bodies were like men . . .

Habib, his clear mirror pressed tight to the mirror of his telecontact beside her in the tent, heard. He asked:

"What are those words, Mara?"

"He was a poet in my own country, Sweden," she thought. "But he never lived in his own country, inside his mind. He lived in the East—in your East, Habib. He sang about the desert of the soul before it became real for a starcruising world."

"What was this man's name?" A hint of sincere curiosity reverberated in the question.

"Gunnar Ekelöf. He lived in the twentieth century—but inside his mind he lived in another time. Thank you, Habib, for showing me this desert. I understand his poems now . . ."

Then the mirrors were flying apart. Wind rushed out of the torn drum. They were both back in the desert outside the tent again, forced to fly home to their bodies. The sailors had climaxed. Their energy was vented. Their own commune helmets were switching the experience off. Time was up.

Mara and Habib flew back across the desert of golden dunes to the lonely, isolated caravan of the *Subrahmanyan Chandrasekhar*—a single camel plodding far out on the sand of stars . . .

As Mara woke up on the couch, the two sailors were already exiting from the trance room, grinning sheepishly. Spurning her tenderness, Habib was his dirty urchin self again.

Mara went back to her tiny cabin to weep her bewilderment.

Mara was Swedish for "little witch." But it was also Swedish for "nightmare" . . .

One month out from Earth, there'd been a discussion in the lounge about the Black Hole and the nature of the creature trapped in it . . .

"When we get there, we can fire particles into the ergosphere," Kurt Spiegel explained to an impromptu audience. "This ergosphere is the region between the so-called 'surface of infinite redshift' and the 'event horizon.' 'Infinite redshift' is the outer layer of the Hole, where queer things really start happening. But there is still a possibility of extracting news from there. A particle is fired into the ergosphere; if it breaks up in there, part falls down the Hole, but the other part may pick up energy from the spin of the Hole and emerge into normal space again, where we can measure it. But beyond 'infinite redshift' is the terrible 'event horizon' itself. Geometry collapses, becomes meaningless. Thus there is no longer any way out, since there is *no way*: no way up or down, no in or out, no physical framework. So that's the end of matter, radiation, anything falling in there. I believe we may find out something from the ergosphere—but beyond that, nothing. Anything else is impossible."

"So you believe that Habib is lying about the thing in there?" Liz Nielstrom demanded.

Habib sat silent, face half hidden by the *haik*, though Mara imagined she saw him smile faintly and mockingly.

"Look at it this way, Miss Nielstrom," Carlos Bolam intervened. He was a Chicano physicist who came from a desert region utterly unlike Habib's desert of the mind—from a Californian desert of freeways, drive-ins, hotdog stands, and neon signs. "Thought must be a function of some matrix or matter or organized radiation. It's got to be based on something organized. But by definition there's no kind of organization possible within a Black Hole."

Spiegel nodded.

"All organization is doomed, beyond the event horizon. The name means what it says. Events end there, and that's that. All identity is wiped out, even so basic a difference as that between matter and antimatter. There is only mass and charge and spin—"

"Isn't that sufficient to sustain a mind?" asked Liz Nielstrom, innocently.

Spiegel shook his head brusquely.

"No, even granted a stripped-down kind of existence, this too only lasts a finite time till even this residue is sucked into an infinitely small point. You cannot have a mind organized on a point. That is like angels dancing on a pinhead. Nonsense!"

"I don't know about that," hazarded the fat Ohashi. "Maybe relativistically speaking we can contact this mind for a hell of a long time span, though from its own point of view it is rapidly approaching extinction—"

"But what happens to this collapsed matter when it reaches an infinitely small point, I ask you? I say it must spill out someplace else in the universe. Maybe to become a quasar. Maybe to form diffuse new atoms for continuous creation. This 'being' must *pass through* this hole. He cannot stick there—even if he does exist . . ."

"And you don't believe he does, Dr. Spiegel?"

"I don't think so, no."

"Well, Habib?" Lew Boyd demanded. "What do you have to say to that?"

Habib shrugged.

"We see the universe a different way. I have my symbols, he has his. Did Bu-Psych-Sec think I was lying? That wasn't a casual chat we had about the matter!"

"I suppose not," grudged Boyd.

"So." And Habib retreated back into his robes again.

"If there is a being in there," Ohashi pursued, "he must have some crazy ideas by now. I presume he fell in there by accident; didn't evolve in there. He'll have memories from sometime of a universe of length and breadth and height, but no evidence to back this up, no reliable sense impressions. It'll seem like a mad hallucination, a drug trip. Yet he might just be able to tell us what it's like in there subjectively—"

"To get that information out of Black Hole," snorted Spiegel, "is by definition impossible!"

"Maybe when one of us rides Habib in there—"

"Remember what happened to the sailor who was riding Habib last time? He died in there—and nobody knows why. I'm not riding Habib." Carlos Bolam stared bitterly at the Arab, and Mara thought she caught the hint of another cruel smile on Habib's lips.

"The man wasn't properly prepared for the encounter," Lew Boyd stated ominously. "He thought he was going to meet a mermaid back on Earth, poor bastard. But we'll be keeping a tight eye on the trance this time."

Despite Boyd's grudging acceptance of Habib's story on that occasion, neither he nor Nielstrom showed any sign of trusting the telemedium. It was soon plain to Mara that some trap was being laid for Habib, though if Habib was aware of it he showed no sign of caring.

It puzzled Mara. If Bu-Psych-Sec were so unsure of Habib, why had they sent him out as ship's telemedium yet again? To the same place where a sailor had lost his life!

A couple of weeks after that discussion in the lounge, Boyd and Nielstrom were in there again interrogating the Arab, while Mara stood out in the nacelle, gazing at the redshifting stars receding from the ship and the violetshifting suns ahead of them: suns which she knew as a pure golden desert of dunes—and which she also knew, with a trace of pity, could never be seen as such by the majority of the human race. Perhaps people's crudity and violence were brought on basically by anger at their own limitation of vision?

"You went in there, Habib," she heard.

"In there, there is no 'there,' " said Habib elusively.

"We know all about this collapse-of-geometry business, but you still went *somewhere*."

"True. I went to no-where—"

"If you went to nowhere, perhaps there was *nothing* there?"

"True," smirked Habib. "No-thing."

"How do you make contact with *nothing*, *nowhere*, Habib? That's nonsense!"

"He lives in the midst of non-sense, where even geometry has gone down the drain—"

"*He*? If everything else is so damned uncertain, how can you be so sure of that thing's sex?"

"You have to use some pronoun . . ."

"Why not 'it'? It's only an alien thing, in there. It isn't human, Habib—"

"Even a thing must be allowed some dignity," muttered Habib.

"Interesting point of view," said Boyd.

"I don't see that it'll have much 'dignity'," Nielstrom jibed. "When you isolate a human being in a sensory deprivation tank, he soon starts hallucinating. If you keep him in there long enough, he goes insane. What is the flavor of this thing's insanity, Habib?"

The Arab glanced down at the floor so that the *haik* hid his face.

He laughed.

"What flavor would you prefer? Vanilla? Chocolate? Raspberry?"

"That's not funny," snapped Boyd.

"Oh no, sir, I know how in earnest you are, I remember Annapolis."

"So answer! That being's a psychotic, isn't it? A fragmented mind—"

"Psychosis," said Habib stiffly, "is a judgment within a context. But he has escaped from context. Geometry itself has collapsed. Two and two don't add up to four. The angles of a triangle may be anything from zero to infinity. It's the Navy who are the psychotics, from his point of view."

Habib abruptly raised his head and grinned; he stuck his thumb in his mouth and sucked it like a child sucking a lollipop.

He pulled his thumb out with a plop.

"Chocolate? Vanilla? Raspberry?" He smirked.

"It's all a question of *escaping* from context, isn't it, Habib?" Boyd demanded, furiously accenting that single word "escaping" and outstaring the Arab, till Habib dropped his eyes furtively.

The Subrahmanyan Chandrasekhar changed orbits at 20:00 hours to a circuit as low as they dared fly about the equator of the ergosphere, from where other stars in the sky had their light warped freakishly into long blue worm-like streaks and spirals. But they were still safe enough, orbiting faster than the escape velocity from this zone, flying in a forced curve at great expense of power rather than allowing their orbit to be dictated to them by the local gravity.

Boyd and Nielstrom were waiting for Mara and Habib in the trance room.

"Change of plan," Liz smiled sweetly.

"New procedure," Boyd explained. "Our little witch will inject with 2-4-P-C on her own. You, Habib, will ride with her in—"

"What in the name of—!" Habib recovered himself. "But Mara isn't ready. What a mad thing to do!" He paced up and down between the trance couches in a fury.

"So near and yet so far, eh?" laughed Boyd, enigmatically.

Habib argued; and the more he argued, the more pleased Liz and Lew seemed to be. They taunted him again about the sailor who'd lost his life inside the Hole.

"He poured like water through a sieve, eh, Habib? I wonder if he could have been poured out, deliberately?"

"That's impossible," gasped Mara.

"But think, what if the rider wasn't safe? Just imagine the implications for the Navy."

"A million-to-one accident," mumbled Habib, distraught. "I know I lost a rider in there. But what about the Bu-Psych-Sec man who rode in there after him? He didn't get hurt."

"He was able to switch off in time. He had the Tantric training to hold back from orgasm and withdraw when he saw there was nothing in the mirror at the end. So now you shall ride in there yourself as passenger and let us see what happens."

The Arab stared queerly at Mara.

"*Mekhtoub*," he muttered in Arabic, "it is fated. Poor little witch. May Allah be with you. May you not lose yourself, and me, in there."

"One more thing," added Boyd. "We want to keep in better touch with the medium through the trip." He indicated a slim grey machine, mounted on rubber rollers, backed up against the wall. Tendrils of wire sprouted from it, terminating in tiny suction pads.

"An electromyograph," he said, tapping the machine, "registers the minute voltage changes in the muscles associated with speech. There's always some element of subvocalizing in a trance. It only takes time and money to write a computer programme to make some verbal sense of these electrical effects. So we've finally taken the time and spent the money. The electromyograph processes its data through the ship's main computer, so we can hear real-time speech."

Lew Boyd patted Mara in a patronizingly amiable way.

"Give us a running commentary, won't you, little witch, while you're navigating your way through . . . whatever it is?"

Habib darted a look of horror at Mara—a horror she shared.

"Voyeurs!" cried Habib. "You vile peepers. That's the only privacy we have, our symbol land-scape. That's our only dignity."

"A pilot scheme," smiled Boyd ingratiatingly, his hand lingering on Mara's shoulder. "It's our job after all . . . to know."

There was no golden desert visible now . . .

One great dune was all she could see—curling over at the top like a frozen Hokusai wave. The Black Hole warped her mind's view of the desert into this single, vast, static lip of sand . . .

No wonder Habib hadn't been able to find his way to Earth when this thing hung nearby, dominating the whole field of vision. Where stars were normally spread out as endless ripples of sand, the Black Hole was a whole warped desert in itself.

She hovered by a pure mirror pool, beneath the overhang of that awful cliff, and realized she was already at the event horizon, seeing the symbol of it in her mind.

The sand dune seemed to be falling in on her perpetually, like a breaker crashing, but in this frozen landscape of the mind—beyond events—nothing moved. Nothing could move when there was no "here," no "there."

Somewhere inside that blank mirror was the mind she'd been sent to find.

She had the barest sensation of Habib riding her, but couldn't get through to him to ask advice. Telemedium and rider had so little contact. Till now this had been the main consolation in being a

Navy mind-whore. That, and the beauty of the
desert. Now, it was frightening. She was so utterly
on her own.

Another thing made her anxious. Was it she, or
Habib, who was supposed to contact the mind in
the mirror of the pool? Normally, it was the rider
who spoke to rider. But this mirror had no rider in
it. She remembered something Habib had warned
her about . . . the mirror of illusion that reflects
yourself, that can trap you in it . . .

She knew so little and it seemed so strange and
dangerous here.

Shortly afterward, in that timeless stasis, love
dawned for Mara . . .

There was a consciousness—a presence in the
mirror pool. A craving for Otherness. This being
seemed so alone, and could love so deep.

But how could he reach out a hand to her, when
he knew nothing of length and breadth and
depth? She came from beyond the event
horizon—but how could anyone come from
beyond that?

"How can you *be*?" thought the mirror pool.

He couldn't show her his face. His body. He had
none. But he could search in her mind for words
and make her lips whisper them.

Mara, torn away from her Swedish village of
cool forest, clear lakes, goose honk, by Earth's
Naval draft board, hadn't really awakened till
now. The past three months had been such a false,
horrid nightmare.

Words formed as he found the poetry in her
soul. Her words—or the Other's. It didn't matter.

There was emotional identity. And what's another word for that, but Love?

> He cried:
> "Outside, I should like to see
> Your Inside
> Outside, show me your Inside!
> Outside, are you brave enough?"
>
> And she replied:
> "Inside, are you brave?"
>
> He asked:
> "That I should go outside myself
> Who have only myself to be in
> Is *that* what you demand?"
>
> "Yes!" she cried to her lover.

What did those sailors and scientists know of this? With all their brash talk of Surface Velocities equal to the Speed of Light. Of Singularities and Strangeness! What did they know of true Singularity, those trashy men! With their Kruskal Coordinates for Schwarzschild Spacetime, what did they really know! With their tin starship flying outside the Surface of Infinite Redshift, far beyond the Event Horizon—beyond this lonely pool where time had frozen—how could they establish a relationship, locked outside as they were forever?

In the *Subrahmanyan Chandrasekhar*, her body lay in a trance . . .

"The boat goes round and round," she sang,

"In the circles of Day and Night
But never do I lose my grip upon You.
You
Shall be my oar!"

What did those wretched scientists want her to do? Interrogate this being about his state of mind and how he saw physical conditions inside a collapsed star?

"Could I
Describe Height,"

she sang, to taunt the scientists and Bu-Psych-Sec officers, if they were spying on her voice successfully up there,

"I would choose
A star at the head
A star at the feet
And under the feet a mirror-image
Concluding in a star."

They wanted to hear the secrets of a *black* Hole. Yet it wasn't black at all, but a startling pearly white; shimmering, opalescent, surrounded by that yellow lip of sand like a curling shell. It was the color of mother of pearl, set in gold. They wanted to know about Length and Breadth and Height? She sang out:

"Could I describe Breadth
I would choose an embrace

Because I have senses
False and primitive
And cannot grasp what really Exists

There is no Star
Where your head is
There is no middle-point
Where your feet stand
But an inch of your loveliness
I have known."

They wanted to know about distances and measurements? She shouted joyfully at the top of her voice:

"An inch of your loveliness
I have known!"

Mara felt the brush of the being's presence on her lips. And then his image grew clearer—as though he had at last understood how to communicate himself, in his own thought forms rather than in poetry filched from her own mind. He made a clearer and clearer statement of identity. Some of it totally evaded her, presenting itself in mathematical or abstract alien symbols she had no knowledge of—forged according to an alien logic from a region where the laws of logic, and even mathematics, had been radically different from the logics devised by humans to suit a universe of elements coherently bonded together into galaxies, stars and planets. But much came through. And when he failed, his symbols hunted for some other means of resonance within her. Concepts using the raw symbolism of her own

thought processes for internalizing sensations—
tactile, kinesthetic, erotic sensations—took the
place of words then.

In this blend of words and formalized sensations, he coded his message to her, presenting her
with the Black Hole he inhabited as the essential
mode of existence; the shadow cast by which con-
stituted the "solid" universe of stars and planets.

He reversed the Real and the Unreal for her, till
she knew the joy of escape that Habib must have
tasted three years earlier.

"Do you not know that this is the Real, the other
the Unreal? Let me tell you about the origin of
things . . . Mara." His mind reached below her
name for the personal symbol cluster attached to
it. "Dreamspinner . . . Shapechanger . . . Lady
Riding on a Stick Through the Starlit Night . . .

"The Energy Egg exploded before the start of
'things.' (By 'things' I mean stars, starships,
bodies.) It was not the Birth of Things. For a very
short time there was a true physical universe—"
She sensed him searching her mind for measurements of time. "It lasted . . . ten to the minus
forty 'seconds,' by and large, this universe.
Soon—and when I conceive 'soon,' I conceive a
time long before that universe was one 'second'
old—all that would later be 'matter' had already
become a near-infinity of tiny 'black holes.' Space
and Matter march hand in hand. But how could so
tiny a volume of newly created Space contain so
much hatched energy? It could not grow fast
enough. The only way Space could expand
swiftly enough to contain the hatching was by
expanding inwardly, creating a myriad holes.

That was the one and only mode that so much could exist in—holes. Each hole could be no larger than ten to the minus twenty-three 'centimeters'—"

"Numbers so small! I can't *feel* them. They mean nothing."

"And of these tiny holes is all 'matter' made. Atomic particles are only a tightly bonded state of these; and in binding, these holes release huge energies. It was those energies, and their release, that powered the expansion of this thing you call 'universe'—not the hatching of the egg itself. Do you understand, Mara?" A touchless caress indicated the curve of the Hokusai wave, beyond which was a universe of stars, starships, bodies, and matter. "That is only a para-universe—a secondary cosmos you inhabit. You have crossed over into the no-place where Reality is. Another was here. How long ago? He would have joined me but the illusion of matter dragged him back—"

"Habib . . ."

He reached below the name for its symbols: the Bedouin, the pilgrim to Mecca, the escapee from shabby caravanserais . . .

"Yes. It was him. But now you can join me. Will you join me, Mara?"

"Are you . . . God? You say you were there at the creation of things!"

"Is 'God' a creator of 'things'? I left before things began. I am not responsible for things." She sensed anger and frustration. "Things are only shadows cast by knots in the eternal, vital void that the true universe collapsed into. This is what hatched from the egg of being, not *that*, out there.

This is the true purpose of creation, not *that*. So join me, Mara, be free of illusion and be my bride—"

Are you a devil then? she thought fearfully. She stared at the timeless pool, tasted his faceless kisses on her cheeks, his fingerless ruffling of her hair, in that place where the Hokusai wave hung like the ultimate battlement—not penning in the chaos of the Black Hole, but resisting the weak thrust of the silt of matter that had piled up against this mind's domain over aeons of spurious reality; stars, starships, bodies . . .

"But what are you?" she hesitated.

"I am the Lover," the answer came. "The All-embracing. There is no loneliness. But I invite you—"

She remembered the Tantric myth of Shiva and Shakti, the sexual pair so deeply joined in eternal copulation that they did not know of their difference. Shiva and Shakti, united at first, had separated. Shakti had danced the dance of illusion to convince Shiva he was not One, but Many, creating from her womb the world of multiple objects existing in the illusory flow of time. He, then, the Void, played the role of Shakti, to the Shiva of the matter universe which she, and Habib, represented. The fact that in the myth Shakti was woman, and Shiva man, was irrelevant. "He" had been as ready to love Habib . . . as he was ready to love her. "He" was an arbitrary pronoun, at best.

Yet she sensed a terrible danger if she yielded to him, if "solid" matter was to be wooed by the original nothingness at its heart. Perhaps in a few billion years a final copulation of the "Universe" with "Void" was destined to liberate the energy to restart the cycle . . . But so soon—already?

But why should she care about danger to stars and ships and bodies? A surge of joy took hold of her. She could be the first creature of matter to live the Tantric myth right through to its end, and be truly loved, as no one else had, by this being who was not "being."

"You are the Lover; then love me—" she whispered.

And the mind in the Black Hole gathered about. Her lips were brushed, her hair stroked, the palms of her hands traced sensuously.

The Hokusai wave itself began to tremble; not to fall in on her—rather, to roll backward, away from the still pool, towering up kilometers into the void sky . . .

Through a mist she sensed cries, orders—voices tissue-thin and torn like tatters in a storm. For the Black Hole was changing its configuration in space, gathering itself for an assault on Being and Matter; and as charged particles were sucked in toward it they sprayed the danger signal of increased outpourings of synchroton radiation and gravity pulses . . .

As he reached out to embrace her, along the line of her thoughts, tracing the yantric geometry of her teletrance back to its origin in the orbiting starship, dune and pool dissolved, and she was snatched away . . .

They had executed Emergency Return Procedure on her—a violent *coitus interruptus* of chemicals and sheer brute force.

A syringe gleamed in Nielstrom's hand. Habib lay weeping, naked, in a corner of the room, his penis a shrivelled button. He coughed, a thin smear of blood on his lips; hunched over his nakedness and bruises, gathering the energy to reach his *aba* and cover himself. It looked as though some urban vigilantes had caught him raping Mara and beaten him up. Mainly this was the action of the trance-cancel drug whose results showed so dramatically—a massive physiological aversion: cold turkey compressed into seconds. But perhaps, too, some gratuitous violence had been used in wrenching him away from Mara and depositing him there.

Mara hurt so badly that the pain crumpled her into a foetal ball, around a belly raped by withdrawal and not by entry. Her nipples were bee stings mounted on top of cones of soft agony like tortured snails stripped of their shells and teased with burning matches (a flicker image from Lew Boyd's childhood sucked in during the decaying moments of the trance).

Lodwy Rinehart stood there in the room with Boyd and Nielstrom, his face blank stone.

They played tapes of her poetry back at her. The voice was slurred and smeared, barely recognizable as Mara's, but the words were identifiable enough. At least the poetry was.

"May you rot in Hell, Boyd," swore Habib through his tears. "May Allah use your guts for spinning yarn."

"There's no alien being in there, is there, Habib?"

"Of course there's a—a being in there," Mara gasped. "I met him. Touched him—"

"Even fell in love with him," smirked Nielstrom.

Mara couldn't understand what was happening, except that it must be one more cruel effort to humiliate her.

Boyd's lip curled in anger and contempt.

"Did you think you'd fooled us, Habib? But nobody deserts the Navy, mister—but *nobody*! That's what cathexis with home is all about."

He swung round on Mara.

"And as for you, little witch—didn't you suspect what Habib was up to? No, I guess you didn't, or you'd have been more scared for your sanity."

His every word was a slap in her face, so recently brushed by love.

"I don't understand any of it," she moaned. "Leave me alone—leave me to myself."

"Ah there it is! The root of the matter exposed. To be left to yourselves. That's what you'd like, isn't it? But how, eh? You can't trance-trip without a rider. That's where the energy comes from, to jump light-years, the rider's sexual frustrations. You keep him rooted to Earth, he keeps you rooted to the ship. The psychological security of the ship and its whole communication net rely on this interplay—"

Mara wept, at these hateful, bewildering people around her. She cried for the still pool beneath the dune . . .

"Why don't you tell her, Habib?" Boyd sneered. "You're supposed to be her teacher."

"Tell her what? She *knows* what is down there."

"Does she? Shall I tell her what *we* know? There's an event horizon—a one-way membrane into the Black Hole. But what if a mind could perform a balancing act on the very horizon itself, eh, Habib? If you could attach yourself to the standing wave there? No more Navy duty then, Habib—you'd be able to hole up in there and forget about us." He smiled bitterly at his own unintended pun.

"What's this about standing waves, Boyd?" the captain demanded. "Don't make me play guessing games on my own ship."

"It's something we've theorized about at Bu-Psych-Sec, sir. The universe hangs together because of causal relationships. But ever since Pauli, in the twentieth century, scientists have speculated about other, alternative relationships—noncausal ones. Clearly these telemediums function because of this noncausal aspect of things. But with the explosive development of star travel, we've been far too busy exploiting the phenomenon efficiently at Bu-Psych-Sec, and holding society together, to do really deep research. Damn it, we're just fighting to hold the line. You've got to protect society against the disruptive effects of star travel! Well—whereabouts in the universe do you find a tangible physical boundary between the causal and the noncausal?"

"The event horizon," nodded Rinehart.

"On one side is the world of cause and effect," Boyd went on effervescently. "On the other side there isn't any meaningful framework for cause and effect to operate in. Effectively, it's a non-causal zone. We think the friction between the two models of reality generates a kind of standing wave of what I suppose you have to call 'probabilities.' Strange things can happen there. And Habib saw his chance of breaking the causal chains that fasten him to his body and his rider, and the starship, and escaping. But he had to be physically close to the place—and it had to be a two-stage process—"

"Boyd's wrong—there is a Being," gasped Habib. "It's not me."

"Mental mutiny?" growled Rinehart, paying no attention to the Arab's protests. "That's a new one for the book."

"A particularly ingenious crime, Captain. Habib sacrificed that sailor's life force to build himself a matrix for his mind to fix on, in there. In doing so, you could say he had to split his personality. No wonder we found so little of all this in his mind, beyond the glaring desire to escape, back there in Annapolis. Habib had covered his tracks up skilfully, like the furtive Bedouin he is. Part of his mind stayed there at the event horizon, ready to receive the rest of him, the major portion of his consciousness. But the Bu-Psych-Sec officer who rode him that second time had the sense and the training to break the trance. He pulled out, took Habib home. Bu-Psych-Sec decided we'd give him sufficient rope to hang himself. He didn't realize the rope woule be round his ankle restraining him at the critical time! It was no use his being the rider, you see—he couldn't make a transference that way. We'll be most interested to learn his tricks when we strip him down again, and the little Swedish witch has her mind peeled to yield up her memory imprint of that bit of fractured mind she fell in love with. We'll have the full picture then."

Habib's eyes met Mara's urgently, begging her to believe him, not Boyd. Her own mind swam with doubts. Had that only been a simulacrum of Habib she had met in there, and all the symbols telling her of how the universe was *nothing*, only lies—part of a cheap trick?

No—he couldn't have contrived it; couldn't have invented a whole alien presence, a viewpoint that reversed the universe! It had to be real!

Boyd was still talking.

"The most important thing of all to know is *how* Habib did this thing. I don't just mean from the security angle. Once we know how the noncausal force operates in conjunction with the universe of cause and effect, given a stretch of luck we can discover how to build a noncausal stardrive. I feel it in my bones. Imagine instantaneous travel, Captain—the power, the expansion, the *control*! Imagine the whole galaxy in our back yard—and all the other galaxies!"

Lodwy Rinehart could imagine. Still, one thing puzzled him.

"Why did the Hole act up, just then? It's stabilized now. But it expanded by two or three percent in a matter of minutes. If I remember my physics, that should require the swallowing of something of the order of a whole sun—"

"We'll know all about it when we analyze the data, but if you want my snap judgment on that, just remember we were tampering with noncausal forces there, at their physical interface with the causal universe. You can take it as an indicator of the kind of power we'll be able to tap . . ."

They played more tapes, but the poetry degenerated into a verbal mishmash—a semantic white noise that sounded like the very entropy of language itself, except where occasional words and phrases came through, treacherously, twisted out of context.

What Boyd was saying about Habib's "Plot" had to be the maddest fantasy. Perhaps he could be right about harnessing the energy of the void. But he didn't understand the danger. She had known what the danger was, as the alien mind dilated to receive her. They might build themselves a machine that would wreck matter and reality itself, instead of a stardrive. But for all she cared, they could wreck the whole galaxy of stars. Her sex ached so fiercely, and her soul . . .

"Incidentally, Boyd," the captain inquired casually, "what would have happened if you'd sent Habib in there as medium, with his little witch riding him? Do you suppose he'd have sacrificed her to escape?"

"It's not true, Mara," cried Habib. "They are mad, not us. They can't stand the knowledge that all is based on illusion in the universe!" However, he began to giggle stupidly, because the effort of subterfuge—or the effort of explanation—was too much for him (since she *knew* anyway). It was one of the two, but which?

Boyd glanced at her ironically, as Nielstrom slipped a sedative needle into Habib's arm.

"I imagine he was pretty desperate, sir."

"No!" moaned Mara. "It isn't true. You don't know anything."

It wasn't you in there, Habib. It was *Him*. Though I could share with you. He was big enough, my Lover.

They're celebrating in the lounge. Fat Ohashi. The Prussian. The Chicano. Boyd and Nielstrom. Rinehart has spliced the mainbrace in true old Navy style, as we race away from the Black Hole and away from . . . *love*.

The autopsy on my love will be starting soon; the unpeeling of my mind; the final rape.

What shall I do, Habib? Kill myself?

For I've known an inch of loveliness. And an inch is all I'll ever be allowed to know of loveliness.

Little witch.

Big nightmare.

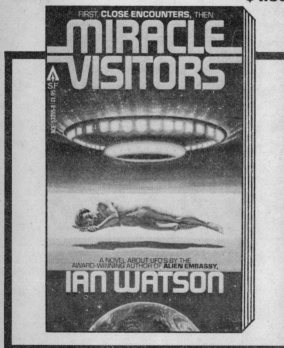

Flandry Is Back!

In February, Ace Science Fiction celebrates the return of Paul Anderson's incomparable **ENSIGN FLANDRY.**

Catch the Flandry fever—read Book I of the Saga of Dominic Flandry: **ENSIGN FLANDRY.** **$1.95**